INTRODUCING ...

Horace
Fox

Charlie
Boom

Loveness
Foxduka

Weasel
Le Hoop

Zigzag
McVitie

Badger
Burnhard

HORACE FOX
IN THE
CITY

Jacqui Hazell

Nowness Books
London

Text & Illustrations copyright © Jacqui Hazell 2020

ISBN 978-0-9957268-4-0

Cover design by Jacqui Hazell

A CIP catalogue record for this book is available from the British Library.

For Z & B

One

Horace Fox was nine months old when his ma threw him out.

'I'm sorry, son,' she said, 'but now you've grown, the time has come for you to leave this place and find your own way.'

Horace looked around at the home he loved. It was only a

covered ditch on scrubland by the railway track, but it felt warm and safe – brown and earthy with a soft layer of dried oak leaves.

'Can't I stay and look after you, Ma?'

'It's what foxes do, Horace, you know that. Your brothers Eddie and George went off weeks ago. You're lucky you've stayed so long.'

'But what about Kitty and May?'

Kitty and May were his sisters, born just moments before him. Surely it wasn't fair that they could stay while he, the youngest, had to leave?

Kitty stifled a sob, while May looked down at her paws.

His ma took a deep breath and Horace noticed her gently swollen belly.

Is there new life growing inside her?

His ma, Rosalie, usually a fine flash of orange-red vixen, normally gave birth to large litters. Horace had been one of six until his brother Bert was taken by a badger on the prowl.

His ma settled down, resting her belly on the ground. 'It's that time of year,' she said. 'I'll be needing your sisters' help.'

Horace understood. There was little room now they were all grown. Winter was here and there wasn't enough food to go round. His elder brothers had offered to go, and it had made life easier. He too should go – he knew that. It was what foxes did.

His ma Rosalie's tail drooped and her eyes welled with tears as she gazed at Horace. 'To think you were the smallest and weakest – how handsome you've become.'

Horace was indeed a striking young fox with his fine long nose, dark amber eyes and a reddish-brown coat with brilliant white fur at his throat and chest.

'I'll miss you, son.'

Horace stroked the wall of the den with his tail. The hard mud was firm and smooth, the sign of a well-loved home.

They had moved there following Bert's terrible death, abandoning the much-loved den in which they had all been born.

Poor Ma – there was no way she could have known what would happen. A starving badger with a wounded paw had wandered into the tunnel and grabbed Bert, who had been closest to the entrance. In a panic, Rosalie had launched herself at the badger, but he had been too strong and had backed out, taking Bert with him.

Horace never saw his brother again and Rosalie had abandoned the den and moved her cubs to the ditch. Horace's dad, Dickie, had come too, but one night soon after he went out and never returned. Horace had often asked for his dad, but Rosalie would only say that Dickie had gone after the badger with the wounded paw to avenge Bert's death.

After that, Rosalie had kept constant guard and the covered ditch became home. But yes, it was too small now they were all grown and a new litter was on the way. It was time for Horace to go.

Forgive me for a moment.' Horace dived to the floor and rolled around in a frenzy, throwing a tornado of dried leaves, dust and mud into the air.

'Has he gone crazy?' Kitty said. 'What's got into him?'

'Horace, stop that!' May said.

Jumping back to his feet, Horace's shiny orangey-red coat was now peppered with oak leaves.

'I just want to take the smell of home with me,' he said. 'I'm afraid I might forget what it's like and I want to remember it always.' Horace sniffed the air, keen to take in that strong musky smell that only a fox can appreciate.

His ma nuzzled him. 'I love you, son.'

His sisters groomed the leaves from his coat and Horace tried to hold it together as he said his goodbyes.

'It's time,' Ma said. 'You must go out and make your own way in the world.'

Tails drooping in sadness, Horace, his sisters and Ma all huddled together for a moment.

'Remember what I told you,' Ma said, 'and beware of sticks. They're not all bad but it's hard to tell either way.'

Swallowing his nerves, Horace nodded. From the moment he was born he'd heard the warnings. Sticks were what they called those tall, upright, two-legged creatures who build everywhere and dump rubbish. He'd always been told they were best avoided.

'And skulk wherever possible. A hidden fox is a successful fox.'

Horace hid behind Kitty. 'Consider me invisible!'

'It's no joking matter,' his ma said, shaking her head. 'Off you go now.'

His sisters nuzzled him, sighing loudly to let Ma know it wasn't fair.

'Come on, girls – let your brother go.'

With his head low and eyes downcast, Horace gave one last slow wave of his bushy tail. 'I'll be on my way then.'

'Be careful crossing those roads!' Ma shouted. 'And avoid the railway track.'

Horace knew the story of poor Uncle Henry so there was no way he'd be taking that route. Instead he cut across the scrubland towards the barbed wire fence along the edge of Ma's territory.

Horace had rarely been beyond that fence.

There was a small jagged hole in the wire. Trembling, he pushed his snout and whiskers through to see if he could make it.

You can do this!

Sucking in his cheeks and belly, he jumped.

'Aargh!' A tuft of red fur caught on the wire, leaving a bare patch of skin on his backside. He felt a little shaky and his fur stood on end.

Pricking his ears, Horace listened to the low-level rumble of traffic. His stomach knotted and he sniffed the air, with its background whiff of choking fumes. All around him stood rows of buildings, lots of them. Horace knew what they were – dens belonging to sticks.

Why would anyone build dens in such an obvious place? It's best not to live where you'll be noticed. Ma says you should live underground and out of sight whenever possible.

Surveying the street, he saw sticks approaching with a box on wheels and there was wailing and the smell of milk.

Is there a stick-cub? No time to find out – you mustn't be seen.

Too late to hide, Horace took the only option left to him. Head down, he raced past all the houses towards a distant patch of green, but as he drew nearer, he realised there was a road in the way. Beyond that road lay grass and trees and beyond that thousands of buildings big and small.

That must be Central Stickland – the big city!

He'd met commuters – foxes that walked a long way each night to go there. Always sleek and well fed, they told stories of strange foods he'd never heard of – noodles, curry, kebabs, fried chicken, chips and round sugary buns with a curious hole. This food was left out for anyone and everyone. They said a black sack was often the sign and sometimes sticks arranged it on the ground in the open air like an offering. The thought made Horace's stomach groan.

Is that where I should go?

His heartbeat quickened and his fur bristled. He preferred the look of the more familiar green land that lay in between. Perhaps he could stay there?

Pausing at a verge, he sniffed the long grass.

What's this? Can it be true?

There was the scent of his brother Eddie and nearby he

could smell George. There was no doubt about it. A fox's fine sense of smell can pick up the faintest trace of a loved one's scent.

Eddie and George came this way. That's lucky! Well, there's nothing to worry about then – I'll be with my brothers in no time.

His brothers had gone before him and now he could follow their trail. It was all quite simple – he would find Eddie and George and life would be good.

Sniffing the ground at the kerbside, he suddenly lost the scent of his brothers and Horace stared open-mouthed at the thundering traffic. He couldn't imagine going any further and yet his brothers must have crossed this very road. If he wanted to find them, then he too would just have to face the same danger.

Even the smallest vehicle appeared deadly.

Horace coughed and his eyes watered.

Why do sticks need such vile machines?

Well, maybe life's a struggle when you only have two legs.

He swallowed hard as an image of poor Uncle Henry, squished to fox-paste on the railway track, flashed in his mind. He had to shake the thought from his head. This was no time for feeling scared. A fox must remain focused.

I must find Eddie and George.

I must cross that road.

But Horace had never crossed a road before, not by himself anyway. His ma had always been there by his side, giving him hard stares that told him to get a move on. But now, for the first time, he had to go it alone. He coughed again, not used to the fumes, as the metal boxes on wheels sped past. There were black square ones, long red rectangles and smaller ones in a whole array of colours.

His innards shook as the vibrations went right through him.

Best get it over with. A fox must go on.

With his ears pricked, Horace looked both ways but the traffic confused him.

How fast would these monsters reach me?

It was hard to judge the speed of the vehicles and again a vision of Uncle Henry – dead on the tracks – flashed through his mind.

Help! I should turn around and forget it – beg Ma to let me stay. But then, what does she always say? A fox should face his fears and if all else fails, run.

Horace looked back at the road.

What's this?

Everything had stopped. The traffic had halted in a neat orderly line. There was a red light on one side, while facing him was a green flashing one in the shape of a stick.

What can it mean?

His eyes wide, he stared at the traffic.

Why aren't they moving?

Every single metal beast had come to a stop.

Right, leg it!

Head down, Horace made a run for it, straight across, in the stylish dash of a young fit fox. Within seconds, he pulled up fast on the other side.

Phew, made it!

Puffing out his brilliant white chest, Horace scurried along the pavement with a bounce to his stride.

I did it! I crossed a road all on my own.

I can do anything.

Two

Strutting along, Horace's pride in crossing his first road alone was quickly forgotten when he looked to his left and saw nothing but high metal railings barring his way.

Can I go over them?

The bars went up in long straight lines leading up to a sharp innards-busting point.

No, not without getting stuck on those spikes!

Poking his nose through the railings, he stared longingly at the lush green fields on the other side. He could smell bugs and hear their scratching and scurrying and it made his mouth water.

A few sticks were ahead of him on the path, so Horace did his best to keep close to the railings.

Silent goes the fox, Ma says.

Skulk, stay low and you'll rarely be seen.

Sticks don't notice much. They don't have sharp senses like we do and mostly they forget to use them.

'Look – a fox!' A stick stopped and gawped at Horace.

They weren't quite as forgetful as Ma said then.

Oops, I'd better run for it!

Pelting along the railings, Horace found a break in the fence and dashed through.

Well, look at that – I found the way in! Don't I always come through in the end?

Making a swift left turn, Horace headed straight for the foot of a large hollow tree. He could hear rustling down there.

Must be beetles, lovely beetles, black, shiny and moving – just the way I like them.

Poking his snout into the hollow, he scooped up a mouthful and their legs twitched in his mouth as he threw his chin up, forcing the wriggling creatures to the back of his throat.

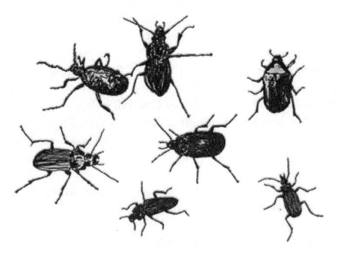

Mmm, crunchy and so very tasty!

He licked his furry cheeks.

Following his nose again, he turned left at the next tree.

Eddie, George, Eddie, George.

They were all he could think about as he searched for their scent on trees, grass and plants.

That bush smells of Eddie, that tree stump smells of George.
He was on their trail, determined to find them.
I'm sure they've not gone far.

Horace soon realised, however, that his brothers' trail was far from simple. Yes, Eddie and George had visited this enormous stretch of green, covering every inch in search of food, it seemed, and Horace found himself criss-crossing the same area several times, circling every tree and sniffing at every bush and patch of soil.

Hours he spent whizzing around, following a trail that seemed endless and eventually his tender young bones began to ache and his paws grew sore.

Eddie, George.

Again he could smell their scent sprayed onto the leaves of an evergreen bush. It was a comfort to him and he sat down and closed his eyes. The grass was springy and soft and reminded him of the leaves that carpeted his ma's warm ditch. Cheered by the thought, his breathing slowed and deepened as he dreamt of wrestling with his brothers in the early morning sunshine at that magical hour when the sticks are asleep.

Hours later, Horace woke to find the world had changed.

Nothing was as it had been.

The sky, the trees and the ground were all white.

Everything was covered with frost, thicker and heavier than any he'd ever seen before.

Looking up, it was hard to tell where the fir trees ended and the sky began.

Is this white stuff snow?

Ma had told Horace how it falls like blossom over the whole world with whiteness as brilliant as the fur on his own chest.

The snow was tail-deep, right up to the top of his legs, and the brightness made his eyes water. Horace shook a layer from his furry bottom and shivered.

It's the wrong time of day for foxes.

It was his first day alone and he hadn't slept long. Daylight made him uncomfortable. Normally he didn't rise until dusk, but something had woken him. He'd been snoring but there'd come a rumble, not thunder but a deep grumble, almost a growl, from deep down in his belly, demanding food soon – straight away – *now!*

Horace pricked his ears, sniffed the air and peered around, keen to catch the slightest movement in the snow. Nothing. The squirrels, birds and even the rats had all disappeared up trees or into their burrows underground. The snow was deep and the ground so hard he couldn't even gobble up a few earthworms.

What would Ma do?

Rosalie never failed to find food.

Trust your senses, Ma says. If you can't smell food or see it, sometimes you can hear it.

Horace pricked his ears and listened.

Something was moving beneath the snow.

There we go!

He leapt up, dived down and re-emerged in a shower of snow with a tiny mole held fast between his jaws. Giving it a little shake, he took a few bites.

Eww!

He made a face. Mole was not his favourite food, rather fusty in taste, but he was in no position to be picky.

Moving on, he again sniffed the ground, searching for his brothers' scent. Nothing. He could no longer smell them.

Eddie, George, where are you?

The sun was low. It would soon be dark. A better time for foxes. He turned towards the city.

Do I take a chance and head off to the bright lights?

Over there beyond the trees he was sure he'd find food. Friends had told him how easy it was, with snacks left out all over the place. He drooled at the thought, spit dripping off his tongue as he dreamt of his favourite treats – fresh pigeon, eggs and earthworms.

The jagged skyline of the city made his heartbeat quicken. What did he know of such a place? It was only hours since he'd left his beloved family and taken his first steps alone. His stomach rumbled, a heavy grumble, so deep it hurt.

If and when there's no food nearby, a fox must move on.

Padding through the deep snow, he headed towards the tall buildings of the city. It wasn't far. Head down, he crossed a bridge and trudged across the frozen land until he reached the edge of the park.

He'd nearly reached the city – or had he?

Horace stopped in his tracks, wide-eyed and open-mouthed at the sight of a road that was far busier, noisier and wider than the only road he'd ever managed to cross on his own. It had many lanes of traffic filled with zooming metal monsters.

Horace's shoulders slumped.

How will I ever cross this?

He waited by the roadside, hoping everything would stop again for him, but his bottom grew numb on the freezing pavement and he realised it wasn't going to work this time.

His stomach rumbled again, so loud it was more like a growl.

I need food now, but how do I cross this road to the land of plenty?

Horace's head hurt from all the thinking. He wasn't used to having to make so many decisions. But then, out of the corner of his eye he spotted something small and grey with a pink whip of a tail dart out from the frozen undergrowth and the smell of rat filled his nostrils. Horace's tongue grew damp with longing and he gave chase.

But what happened? Where did it go?

Somehow the rat had given Horace the slip by disappearing under the road.

Horace followed and found the ground sloping down beneath his paws.

Again he caught sight of the rat. It turned left and Horace did the same, his eyes blinking as he found himself in a bright white tunnel that stank of wee.

Eddie, George – can it be true?

Horace tried to work out if this really was the family scent with top notes of George? There were so many markings it was hard to make out his brothers' glorious whiff amongst the odour of dogs, rats and even sticks.

Horace glanced up. He'd not quite taken in where he was. The ceiling of the tunnel was lined with bright white lights on either side and as a fox he was far too obvious.

Must get through this and out.

Skulking along the left-hand side, he followed the tiled wall all the way through to the end and then dashed up another concrete slope. At the top, in the cold evening air, he looked back and realised he'd once again crossed a road.

Wow, would you believe it – I can even go under them!

On the opposite side he could see the park railings where only a moment before he'd been sitting confused on the frozen pavement, while on this side were mammoth buildings rising up into the black sky, higher than any of the grand old trees he had always admired.

How have these buildings grown so tall?

Maybe they're even older than our ancient oaks back home?

Sticks were up ahead and Horace scurried for cover, running behind a large plane tree whose base had been cemented into the pavement.

'Is that painful?' Horace asked, but there was no answer.

He sniffed at the foot of the trunk.

Hang on a mo' – is that possible? Yep, that's Eddie!

He was sure of it, and there was a faint smell of George on the corner nearby.

Taking a side street, Horace kept his nose to the ground on the trail of his dear brothers.

Suddenly a whirring siren made Horace stop dead in his tracks.

What's that?!

He was glad when it quickly faded, but now some strange white sticky stuff was stuck to his back right paw and the more he pulled away, the further it stretched. Keen to be rid of this icky stickiness, Horace chewed at his foot.

Ooh, that's a strange new flavour but the more I chew the less it tastes. This food is rubbish!

He spat it out and then continued to track his brothers, sure that being with them would make everything right again.

Sniffing at the base of a wall, he came across a large paper cup half-full of a thick pink liquid. Horace dipped in his snout and slurped up the cold milky drink. Holding his head back to suck up the last drops, he found that he'd wedged his snout in too tight. He tried shaking it off, jumping about and flicking his head this way and that until his jerky dance finally flicked the cup off and away.

Whatever you do or wherever you go, check for a way out, Ma said. I must be more careful.

A little further on, he pushed his snout inside a crisp packet to snaffle up the last salty dregs before realising that he'd once again trapped his fine long nose and once more had to flick his head from side to side to break free.

So much left out for me on every corner. What's a growing fox to do?

At least the sore ache of hunger had gone from his belly, so he carried on following the scented trail of brotherly love.

Wait – hold on a minute . . .

All of a sudden, Horace looked up. He'd taken a left and kept going, nose to the ground, but where were his brothers leading him? Noise, light and laughter were growing ever louder. This street pointed towards a crossroads that burred with the churn of giant metal monsters, coloured red. Horace watched them pass in a steady stream with only the occasional break. He was still at a safe distance, but his heart was beating faster now. Crowds of sticks were walking in all directions, while above them lights hung from the buildings and across the road like a glittering avenue of trees through which the metal monsters could pass.

Horace looked for a route underground or perhaps a rat who could show him the way? But there was no rat, no underpass and no safe route.

I can't go where my brothers went.

Horace's head hung low and his tail drooped between his legs. The way ahead was no longer clear. He was going to need to think for himself and it wasn't easy. His head throbbed.

So what now? What would Ma do?

Horace looked down at his cold sore paws and sighed.

What else could he do but turn and walk away in the opposite direction?

Already his joy over the milkshake and crisps was fading and his belly was aching all over again. He shook himself to fluff out his coat against the chilly wind blowing down the frozen streets. Staying out of the lamplight, he stuck to the shadows and padded on, one hungry young fox, lost and all alone.

Three

Head bowed and tail low, Horace no longer knew which way to turn – until he picked up the scent of his first takeaway.

Whoa, that smells good!

His tongue dripping in anticipation and head and tail up, he quickened his pace, following his nose around the backstreets.

The sweet aroma grew stronger and he ran along the back of a row of terraced shops to a dark and dirty backyard stacked with boxes and a large silver bin.

That smells incredible!

Horace's eyes widened and he licked his lips, but the bin was far too tall for him to jump straight in.

What now?

There was nothing else for it. Taking a run up, he jumped onto a cardboard box which half crumpled beneath him and then vaulted up onto a short wall. The smell of warm spicy meat was growing stronger.

Maybe it's squirrel? I do love squirrel. One more leap should do it. One, two, three –

Horace dived in over the edge of the large bin.

Instantly there was a snarl and a flash of deadly sharp teeth at Horace's throat.

Leaping backwards, Horace roared in self-defence until he realised who it was. 'Charlie, stop! It's me – Horace.'

Still baring his teeth, the other fox paused and then slowly drew his lips back down over his fangs. 'Horace, you numbskull, what are you doing, jumping me like that? I could've killed you. In fact, I nearly did.'

Horace had landed right on top of his old friend Charlie Boom. Now, Charlie was a great fox but you wouldn't want to get on the wrong side of him. The Booms were a well-known family of tough city foxes, also from the scrubland by the railway track until they moved to the city in search of food. Now they were thriving, surviving even in the worst winters while remaining well fed and well dressed in the longest, flashiest fur coats, with the bushiest tails and brightest white teeth. (Though Charlie's teeth were far from perfect as his left front fang had a chip, after a grisly and rather famous fight with a badger.)

'Horace, well I never – you've finally made it into town!' Charlie smiled, showing a glimpse of that chipped tooth. 'What's happening, bro?'

'You have no idea. I'm so hungry. I thought it was supposed to be easy to find food here. What've you got? Tell me there's something.'

'Oh sorry, mate, you're too late.' Charlie looked down at a plastic container and its last smear of yellow sauce. 'If I'd known you were coming, I'd have saved you some.' Charlie Boom looked down at his tight full belly. 'Oops, excuse me! Boom by name, boom by nature,' he said. 'Better out than in.'

Normally Horace would have laughed, but instead he bit the inside of his cheek, not wanting his own hunger to make him cry in front of his friend.

'What's that?' Charlie froze.

'What's what?'

'That noise, that growling – was that you?'

'I can't help it.'

'Oh look, mate, there's no need for that. It was only a bit of chicken curry. It was almost nothing. Let's not fight over it.'

'Who said anything about fighting?'

'You – you're growling. I know when I'm on rocky ground.'

'I can't help it, Charlie, it's my belly. I've barely eaten a thing since I left home.'

'So what have you had?'

'Only a few beetles, a mole and some strange chewy stuff that stretched.'

'Mole? You must've been desperate, mate. Well, there's plenty of food around. Just follow me and we'll have you sorted in no time.' And with that Charlie Boom led the way out of the bin and back to pounding the icy pavements.

'Smell that? It's fish 'n' chips, food of the gods.' They

scooted around the back of yet another takeaway establishment. Cod in batter, deep fried sausages, soggy chips and mushy peas – the smells hung on the air and yet all the foxes could find was a small puddle of spilt cooking oil.

Horace's eyes welled up. His belly ached that much.

'Disappointing, I know,' Charlie said, 'but don't worry, the options are endless. That's what makes city living so fantastic!' He ran on and Horace followed, though his energy was so low he feared he couldn't go much further.

Cutting across a patch of green at the centre of a garden square, Charlie dived beneath a bench, causing rats to flee in every direction. Neither fox caught a bite.

'Keep your eyes peeled,' Charlie said. 'There are rats everywhere.'

But word had got out amongst the rat community.

'I can't find any,' Horace said. 'It's hopeless.'

'Forget it, let's try down here.' Charlie's nose pointed towards yet another side street, from which came the unmistakeable sound of sticks.

'Wait – it's too dangerous,' Horace said, though his stomach rumbled in disagreement.

'Do you want to eat or what? You don't get nothing without taking the odd risk in life, my friend. Sounds to me like you're desperate, and desperate foxes do desperate things.' And with that, Charlie nipped around the back of a large red-brick building with a painted sign of a dog and a fox.

'I don't like that. Dogs and foxes have never been friends,' Horace said.

'Chill out, bro, it's only a sign for one of them places where sticks meet.'

They heard singing. Horace struggled to make out the words. It went something like: '*We three kings of orange tar*'.

'Watch him.' Charlie nodded towards a stick with a gold

paper crown on his head. The stick was unsteady on his feet and needed to grab hold of the metal railings for support.

'What's the matter with him?'

Charlie shrugged. 'Sticks get like that sometimes, especially after dark.'

The stick swayed and his head wobbled until it seemed he could hold it up no longer. Bent double, he made a strange throaty sound.

'Oh my days, that is beautiful.' Charlie's nose pointed to a yellow lumpy soup-like splurge. 'Smells like curry.'

'I've never had curry.'

'You'll love it. Let's just hope no one else has seen.' They looked all round – no other eyes glowing in the dark. They just had to wait. With difficulty, the stick pulled himself up as straight as he could and staggered away, shouting, 'Merry Christmas, everyone!'

'Let's go!'

Horace smiled for the first time in ages as they dashed towards the lumpy yellow puddle.

'You tuck in, my friend.' Charlie stood back to allow Horace to take his fill, but it smelt so good, too good, and he couldn't help joining in. Licking the ground furiously, it took only a minute for the foxes to clear away every last lump of the yellowy soup. Tongues out, they polished that section of grey pavement to a proper shine.

'Oh Charlie, I feel so much better.'

'That's good, mate. Look, I'd better get cracking, do me rounds and check me territory, know what I mean? Great to see you though – keep in touch.'

'You're going?'

'Things to do, mate.'

'Wait!' Horace tried to keep him talking. 'Have you seen my brothers, Eddie and George? I mean, you've visited Ma's den so you'd know their scent if you smelt it, right?'

But Charlie wasn't listening, not to Horace anyway. His ears were pricked sharp as he scanned the icy streets.

'What is it, Charlie?'

'Shush!'

Horace looked at his older and wiser friend, trying to work out what was going on. 'You're scaring me. What is it?'

Charlie's eyes narrowed. 'Don't look now,' he said out of the corner of his mouth, 'but I think we're being watched.'

Horace, not knowing any better, immediately looked, of course.

'I said *don't look*!'

But it was too late. Horace had seen a figure lurking in the shadows and with his heart racing, he shouted, *'Run!'*

Four

Their heads down, Horace and Charlie were streamlined streaks of red against the grey of the city's pavements as they quickly gathered speed.

Charlie took a sharp left turn and Horace followed, throwing a worried glance over his shoulder.

'Who is that?' Horace said, his voice cracking.

'Don't look, it doesn't matter – just keep running.'

'Who is it? Who's following us?'

'There's a little weasel and someone else, I'm not sure who. Don't worry about it, just keep running.'

'But weasels are country folk. Maybe they're lost and we should help?' Horace said, slowing his pace.

'Run – keep going! We need to get away from here.'

'But it's only a weasel . . .'

'It doesn't matter, I've got bad vibes. We need to shift it – run!'

Again Horace looked over his shoulder. The small furry weasel was racing to catch up, and there was someone else, someone black and white, long and thin, with a black zigzag pattern down its back.

Horace gasped and his heart beat faster. *'There's a snake!'*

'I know,' Charlie said. 'Head down and shift it.'

'You knew?'

'Yes, but I didn't want to alarm you. Come on, move it – do one!'

'Oh my word, I've never met a snake before. Is it dangerous?'

'It's a snake – of course it's dangerous!'

'Change direction, take another street, see if they follow.'

'They'll follow.'

Swiftly they turned left onto a grand square with tall white townhouses.

'Still there, are they?' Charlie said.

Yes, they were, and just passing the statue that Charlie and Horace had passed only a moment before. The weasel was a lean flash of energy fast approaching, whilst the slight slippery snake slid superfast alongside.

'Down here.' Charlie took a right, and right again, then a left, a right and a left. They had moved away from the elegant side streets and squares and were now running past ginormous buildings next to a wide road with many lanes of speeding traffic.

Almost out of breath, Charlie paused. His big city diet wasn't helping.

'Come on, Charlie, they're gaining on us!' shouted Horace.

They were by a grand building ten storeys high. The doorman, in top hat and tails, was holding the door for a thin female stick who was wearing a coat with a red fur trim.

'Don't look,' Charlie said. 'I said, "*Don't look*"! Do you ever listen?'

Horace pulled a face. 'Her coat smells of dead fox. Why would she wear that?'

'You can't think about it, not now.' Charlie glanced back. The short-faced weasel was nearly upon them, with the snake a little further behind. '*Hurry!*'

Cars raced past, their exhaust fumes at fox-level, making Charlie and Horace splutter and rasp as they ran on.

Horace said, 'So where now?'

'I know, down here.' Charlie took a right and ran down

into another subway.

'I've been in one of these tunnels before,' Horace said, but Charlie wasn't listening. Bounding up the far slope they were once again by the park. 'It's so lovely here and there are oodles of fresh crunchy beetles,' Horace added. But Charlie had no time for landscape and shrubs or wriggly snacks. Instead, he kept to the edge, following the perimeter before he ventured down yet another concrete ramp.

This subway was different. There was noise and bustle and the smell of metal coming through an archway to the right.

Charlie pushed forward without looking back.

'What is that?' Horace ground to a halt just as Charlie jumped straight onto a moving metal staircase. 'Oh my word, it's alive.'

Horace stared at Charlie as he travelled down and away.

'Wait, where are you going? Don't go without me.'

'Jump on,' Charlie shouted.

'But it's moving!'

'It'll be fine, trust me.'

Horace glanced behind him – the snake and the weasel were right behind! He took a deep breath and jumped onto the moving metal steps.

It smelt of oil and dirt and he was worried his legs would get caught at the edges. His stomach lurched and he held his breath.

'Hey look – there's a fox on the escalator!' shouted a stick who was travelling up on the next staircase. Other sticks pointed small boxes at Horace.

Please don't shoot!

Horace stood very still and straight, doing his best not to wobble as the metal steps travelled down. It was all so strange but surprisingly smooth and not that bumpy. Even so, something didn't feel right and as he jumped off at the bottom, he realised what it was. The ground shook with a heavy and familiar rumble. 'I know that horrible sound . . .' The fur on the back of his neck stood on end and a sick feeling rose in his throat as he remembered poor Uncle Henry.

'I can't go any further,' he said. 'We're in serious danger!'

Charlie was waiting at the bottom, ready to ride a train. 'Come on, mate, they'll never catch us if we jump on sharpish and travel a few stops. Trust me, I've done it loads of times. It's no problem.'

Horace looked pained. 'Didn't I tell you about Uncle Henry? He mistimed the crossing. All we heard was the train and then the thud. Ma ran out but poor Uncle Henry didn't stand a chance. Fox-paste he was.'

'That's terrible. You should have said, but . . .'

'I can't go on a train. They're dangerous and evil and I promised Ma I'd never go anywhere near trains or train tracks.'

'From what I've seen I'd say cars are worse, but I hear what you're saying.'

They turned and took the moving metal staircase back up. On their way, they spied the weasel and snake heading down on the other side.

'So long, suckers!' Charlie shouted.

'Shush, Charlie, you'll only make things worse,' Horace said, catching sight of the snake's black and yellow eyes. Never had another living creature stared at him so coldly. Horace shook and a fearful shiver ran down his spine.

'Watch your backsss, garbage-eatersss,' hissed the snake. 'We're onto you and it won't be long.'

At the top of the escalator, the foxes took another underpass beneath the mad swirl of the huge roundabout before running up concrete steps to street level.

'This way.' Charlie followed a slush-covered pavement spread with grey grit alongside a very high brick wall. 'I'm guessing your ma told you how almost everywhere is open to us foxes. It's our one advantage. Plus we're great at finding food in bins. We're champion recyclers. Anyway, there's a hole I know near here and it's not quite the front door exactly, but it's handy.' Charlie sniffed his way along the edge of the wall, near the ground. 'Here we go – this is it.' He squeezed his body as flat as it would go. 'Breathe in, my friend.'

This was some hole. Horace and Charlie had to pass under a fence, barbed wire and brick, so they tucked in their bellies to stay as skinny as possible as they inched forward, only to howl in pain when a crackle and a zap suddenly threw them both up and out in the air on the other side. The fur of their coats stood on end and little trails of smoke rose from the ends of their tails.

'Blow me, I'm frazzled!' Charlie said.

Horace blew on the end of his blackened tail. 'Same here.'

'Sorry, mate, I clean forgot to mention – this fence is electric.'

'My ma loves my tail, or at least she did when the end was white and fluffy.'

'It'll recover, but in the meantime consider it a disguise. That snake won't be searching for a couple of foxes with burnt black tails.' Charlie blocked up the hole behind them with broken branches and an old deckchair embroidered with a gold crown and a royal crest. 'With any luck they'll lose the trail,' he said. 'Either that or they'll get zapped as well. I like the thought of that – toasted weasel and chargrilled snake!'

'Wow, what is this place?' Horace's eyes widened as he took in the scene. It looked like countryside with clipped shrubs, lots of trees and a huge spread of snow-covered lawn. The foxes left the undergrowth and passed through a copse of trees to a frozen lake with a small island facing a huge pale stone building that looked like an iced cake made for giants.

'We'll scoot through and leave on the far side,' Charlie said.

'But it's so lovely! Can't we rest a while?'

Charlie frowned. 'I don't think so. It's best we keep going. Never underestimate a slippery snake or a wily weasel.'

They walked across a lawn the size of a field and around the edge of the grand stone building.

Suddenly there was barking. They'd set the dogs off.

Hackles up, Horace paused. 'That sounds like a big pack to me.'

Yellow light was shining from the patio doors at the back of the building, showing the outlines of a dozen short stubby dogs, all of them jumping up, barking and gnashing their teeth.

'We need to get out of here fast!' Charlie said.

Keeping as low as they could, they crept along the side of the building.

Ahead of them were lots of sticks dressed in black and carrying weapons.

'Do you reckon this place is important?' Horace asked nervously.

Everywhere they looked were tall iron railings and guards.

'I don't think we can squeeze through those,' Charlie said with a frown. 'Hold on, the gates are opening – we can nip through if we're quick.' Head down, Charlie went for it, weaving past the security guards and making a dash for a gap that was opening up between the tall metal gates.

'Ha, did you see that?' one guard shouted to another.

'Foxes are vermin – we should shoot it,' said the other one, just as Horace was running past after Charlie.

'Wow, another fox!' a stick laughed, while a sleek car entered the gates, driven by a stick in gloves and a smart cap. Horace took his chance and nipped between the car and the gates. Looking up, he saw a stick peer out of the back window of the car. She was wearing a crown and she smiled and gave a little regal wave as he made his way safely through.

'Ready, steady, go!' Charlie said on the other side, and they raced across a curved road towards a park.

'Phew!' Horace said. 'I can't believe how many roads I've crossed recently.'

'No sign of that weasel or snake,' Charlie said. 'Things are looking up.'

'I'm a teensy bit peckish, what with all that running,' Horace said.

'Seems like you're always hungry.'

'I'm a growing fox. How about another curry then? I liked that.'

Charlie grinned. 'What do you say to a Chinese?'

'Chinese? I've never had Chinese.'

'You've never had crispy duck, pancakes and plum sauce? Let me treat you to a taste sensation, my friend!' Charlie sniffed the air. 'For the love of stir-fry, you're never far from a Chinese takeaway in Stickland – everyone loves Chinese food.'

Horace paused because he'd smelt something else. 'That's Eddie,' he said, nodding towards the corner of a wall. 'I can smell my brother. I'm back on their trail.'

Horace and Charlie sniffed together and soon picked up George's scent too. They followed the trail across a large square and up a hill, past buildings covered in bright lights, and then down a side street, to a concrete ramp leading underground.

Horace sniffed the air in front of them. 'This way – it's this way.' The ramp took them down into a floodlit world below street-level. 'It looks like a den for those metal monsters.'

They found themselves in an underground car park, and to Horace's surprise the "metal monsters" didn't seem at all scary once they were silent and still with their engines turned off.

Horace took another ramp down to an even lower level, where amongst the scent markings of sticks, mice and rats he could still smell Eddie and George. 'They can't be far.' His heart fluttered. 'I can't wait to see them.' The scent trail was so strong he was sure he was about to find them. 'This is it – this must be them.' He stopped at a thick concrete pillar and looked around. 'I don't understand. Where are they? Why aren't they here?'

'Maybe they were sleeping under one of the cars but then moved off?'

Horace's shoulders slumped and his tail drooped to the ground.

'Or maybe they've just gone out to eat?' Charlie said.

'Yes, of course, that's it. They can't be far – we'll follow their trail back out.'

The foxes wound their way back up the ramps of the car park to street level, where they ran past cinemas, burger bars and hot dog stands and then dodged down a dark alley to the rear of a large white building.

Horace shook his head. 'I don't get it. I've lost them.' He sniffed at the walls, several cars and a mountain of bin bags. 'There's a trace of Eddie on the ground over here but it doesn't go anywhere. I don't understand.'

Charlie looked away.

'What is it?' Horace said. 'You look serious.'

'It's nothing.'

Horace stared at his friend. 'You think something bad has happened here?'

Again Charlie looked away.

'You reckon this is where the trail ends?'

Charlie closed his eyes.

'Oh no, please no. Surely they've just gone somewhere else.'

'Well, it's possible,' Charlie said.

'But you don't think so?'

'I don't know.'

'You do think something bad has happened, I can tell. My brothers have gone. Vanished like some giant bird has lifted them up and carried them off.' Horace's shoulders slumped and his tail hung as low as it could go.

'I'm so sorry,' Charlie said, 'but we'll just have to keep going.'

'What's the point?'

Suddenly there was a crash as a door slammed and sticks dressed in white poured from the back of the building.

The foxes fled down the nearest side street until Charlie came to a sudden halt. He leant against a wall to catch his breath, while Horace's tail drooped with disappointment.

'I'm sorry you didn't find your brothers,' Charlie said.

Horace stared down at his paws. 'I was so looking forward to seeing them again.'

'I know.'

'What if they've been harmed?'

'I'm sure there's a simple explanation. Maybe they've gone off somewhere in some way we haven't come up with yet.'

'I don't know.'

'They could turn up.'

Horace sighed. 'I have a nasty feeling something's not right.'

'Oh come on, mate, you can't give up already. Your brothers wouldn't want that.'

'I guess not.'

'There's still hope, and in the meantime you've got me.' Charlie straightened up and twitched his nose. 'Take a sniff of that, my friend. That's stir-fry – the unmistakeable smell of stir-fry.'

'What a delicious scent.' Horace licked his lips. 'It smells good.'

'Doesn't it just? Let's find it.'

They followed the aroma down several streets, across a road, and around a corner where they came to a narrow street hung with red lanterns and neon signs of lucky cats, dragons and pandas.

'I love this place,' Charlie said. 'I always get a good feed in Chinatown.'

After walking through a carved red gateway, Horace stood open-mouthed and staring at a window filled with spit-roasted ducks.

Charlie was gazing up at a lit-up sign of a panda eating noodles over the neighbouring restaurant. 'This is Panda Garden, one of my favourite eateries.'

The foxes skulked off down a side alley to its backyard.

Duck carcasses, half-chewed spare ribs, special fried rice and a generous spill of barbecue sauce – the foxes had chanced upon a feast!

'City living is certainly better since I met up with you.' Horace licked a moustache of barbecue sauce from his face.

'Pity we didn't find any plum sauce – I like a bit of plum sauce.' Suddenly Charlie's ears pricked and he froze, as once again his face wore that dangerous super-alert look, the one that made Horace hold his breath with nerves.

'What is it, Charlie?'

Charlie gave Horace a warning look to be quiet before leaping up and pouncing down on a shadowy figure lurking by the side of the wall.

Weasel!

Charlie had caught the weasel and had him by the throat.

Charlie snarled, making Horace trip backwards over some old noodle boxes.

'What do you want, weasel?' Charlie's one and a half fangs flashed white in the moonlight. The weasel with its short face and small ears made a pathetic choking sound.

Horace edged forward. 'Why are you following us?'

The weasel coughed and twisted his long body and short legs as he tried to escape Charlie's grip, but Charlie was having none of it. He tightened his hold on the weasel's throat.

'Please, sir, release me – let me go.' The weasel's eyes bulged as he dangled from Charlie's jaws. 'I mean you no harm. It's good news I bring, honest.'

Charlie snarled again. 'When has a weasel ever been honest? You don't even know the meaning of the word!'

'That's quite unfair. I'm a respectable creature, I can assure you.' The weasel wriggled and writhed and kicked out but Charlie held him firm.

Horace frowned as he looked the weasel over. 'Why are you sneaking around and following us then? Who are you?'

'Please, if you'd just both relax a little, I could talk.' The weasel squirmed and fidgeted as he tried to ease his long body away from Charlie but it was impossible.

'So who's the snake?' Charlie said. 'Why are you with him?'

'Good news – it really is good news.'

Charlie shoved the weasel up against the wall. 'Whoever heard of good news? I've lived long enough to know there's no such thing.'

'You're quite mistaken, sir. I bring extremely good news for a Mr Horace Fox.'

'I repeat, who are you?' Charlie said.

The restaurant's panda sign flashed overhead, bathing the animals in a red neon light.

'My name's Weasel Le Hoop and I bring very good news for Mr Horace Fox.'

Charlie looked askance. 'Well, in that case, I'm Horace Fox. Let's hear this good news. I could certainly do with a little sunshine in my dark and grubby city life.'

Horace moved closer. He'd waited all his life to hear something good (though some might say nine months isn't so awfully long to wait).

The weasel wriggled and squirmed, rasped and squealed, still trapped eyeball to eyeball between Charlie's strong jaws. 'It is good news, yes,' he squeaked, his bulging eyes leaking tears, 'but I suppose if I think about it, it's both good news and bad news . . .'

'Now we're getting somewhere closer to the truth,' Charlie said.

'Can you just tell us what this is all about?' Horace had a headache from all the tension.

The weasel frowned. 'Which do you want first then – the good news or the bad?'

'Any news will do at this rate because I've had quite enough of waiting to hear what all this is about.' Charlie stared into the weasel's eyes. 'My jaws are feeling a little achy right now and I could easily chomp down and snap them shut – and you know what that would mean, don't you?'

'Oh no, please, sir, don't do that, I beg you.' The weasel's small head was soaked with Charlie's slobber. 'Can you please confirm which one of you good fellows happens to be Mr Horace Fox?'

The foxes looked at each other and Horace shrugged. He wasn't sure it would be a good idea to reveal his identity to this wily stranger.

'Well, who wants to know?' Charlie said, a bobble of spit dripping from his chipped left fang.

'Um, could you ease off a little, kind sir? My throat is feeling awfully tight right now.' The weasel made a pathetic raspy noise.

'I'll release you when I'm good and ready, or maybe I won't release you at all. Things are not looking good for Mr Weasel Le Hoop right now, that's for sure.'

Horace tried to calm the situation. 'One of us may or may not be Horace Fox. It's really none of your business.'

Charlie nodded, giving the weasel a little warning shake. 'You don't need to know nothing about us, weasel. You're in no position to ask. We do the asking and we want to know what this is all about?'

'Right you are, just as you please,' the weasel sighed. 'The good news is that a Mr Horace Fox has been left a very swish den to live in. The bad news is that Mr Horace Fox's father is sadly no more. He has left this wonderful world of the living. He's dead and gone, as it were.'

Horace thought hard, trying to remember his father's face. It had been a very long time since he had last seen him. '*Who* has left this "very swish den"?' he said.

'Well, Dickie of course – Dickie Fox. You don't know the name?'

Horace felt himself redden, embarrassed that he barely remembered his own father. Luckily, thanks to the red fur, only foxes actually know if they're blushing.

'But surely this inheritance should be split between all of

Dickie's young?' Horace thought how his life had begun as one of a litter of six, before poor little Bert was taken by the badger with the wounded paw.

The weasel shook his head. 'No, not so. It is our custom under Natural Law that a property is passed down to the eldest son of a family. It's the only way to make sure it all stays together.'

'Oh well, in that case, it's Eddie you want. He's the eldest.' Horace's heart lightened, expecting the weasel would now help him find his brothers.

'Ah well, as I understand it, that is no longer the case . . .' the weasel said.

A big lump rose in Horace's throat. 'What do you mean?'

'Oh dearie me, this is awkward,' the weasel said. 'Have you not heard?'

'Heard what?' Horace's head throbbed with a dull heavy pain.

'I was informed of a road traffic accident. Nasty – very nasty.'

'Nasty?'

'I'm afraid they didn't stand a chance.'

'*They* – you mean Eddie *and* George? Both of them?' Horace let out a loud sob and then collapsed as if he too had been hit by something hard.

'Just look what you've done! Have you no heart?' Charlie dropped the weasel and darted over to Horace. He nuzzled Horace's cheek till he opened his eyes, and then dived back across the yard, snapping his jaws firmly around the weasel's spindly neck. 'Not so fast, weasel! I want the truth, the whole truth, or I swear your days of weaselling will be well and truly over.'

'Please be reasonable, kind sir. None of this is my doing.'

'What do you mean?' Charlie said. 'There's something you're not telling us and this is your last chance to say what it is before I really lose it with you!'

'Oh, very well,' Weasel Le Hoop sighed. 'The property has been left to him, that much is true, but Mr Horace Fox must claim it fast. There are only five days left for him to do so, but if it's not claimed the den will be up for grabs.'

'Up for grabs?'

'Someone else will take it.'

'Like who?'

The weasel shrugged. 'It's hard to say. These dens, especially the swish ones are extremely desirable. They get taken by others.'

'Who sent you?'

The weasel looked from Charlie to Horace and then back again, his brow deeply furrowed. 'Badger Burnhard,' he said with a tremble in his voice. 'It was Badger Burnhard.'

Charlie's eyes widened and he looked grim. 'Badger Burnhard, the dirty rotten, ruthless business-badger?'

'Yes, that's the one, the very same.'

'What does that murderous greedy lowlife want now?'

'He wants the den of course – the den that has been left to Mr Horace Fox.'

'Doesn't he already own umpteen dens, setts and burrows?'

'Yes, yes, he does. In fact, I do believe he owns twenty, or maybe even more.'

'So then why does he want another?'

The weasel shrugged as best he could in the circumstances without scraping his shoulders on Charlie's sharp teeth. 'Badger Burnhard always wants more, that's just the way he is. He can never have enough.'

'So that greedy heartless badger wants the den,' Charlie said, 'and he wants to stop Horace claiming it in time? And so far both Eddie and George are out of the picture. Was that Badger Burnhard's doing?'

The weasel bit his lip and looked elsewhere.

'Afraid to look me in the eye?' Charlie stared at the weasel.

The weasel's eyes bulged. 'No, sir, of course not.'

'And why is the snake following us?' Horace asked.

The weasel swallowed hard. Whatever it was, he was too afraid to say.

Charlie's jagged left fang nibbled at the weasel's throat. 'You're looking mighty uncomfortable, I must say. It's not good for your health keeping secrets, so let's have it, weasel – what's the answer and make it good!'

Again the weasel swallowed. 'Have you heard of Zigzag McVitie?'

Charlie shoved the weasel against the wall. 'What are you telling me, you nasty stringy piece of meat?'

The weasel fretted as once again he found himself eyeballed by Charlie.

'Are you telling me that *Zigzag McVitie*, also known as the Striped Assassin, has been hired to take out first Eddie and George and now *Horace?!*'

The weasel gave the smallest, slightest nod.

Horace trembled. He was hot and his head hurt from all the stress and arguing. 'Who is Zigzag McVitie?' he said, his voice a whisper.

'He's a deadly killer, that one, with many successful contracts to his name,' Charlie said grimly. 'They say he injects venom through his razor-sharp fangs and can shoot to kill from five metres. A single bite is enough to make your body swell up and die.'

Just what he did *not* want to hear – Horace turned to fox-jelly and had to sit down fast, his legs almost giving way beneath him. This Zigzag McVitie was bad news all right.

Charlie looked at the weasel. 'So is that what happened to Eddie and George? Did McVitie get them?'

'I honestly have no idea.' Again the weasel looked shifty.

'Hold on,' Charlie said, 'snakes hibernate – shouldn't McVitie be wrapped up all cosy and warm, snoozing away the winter in his viper's nest?'

'As I understand it, he's come out of hibernation especially.'

'Especially?'

'Badger Burnhard made him an offer he couldn't refuse.'

'Like what?' Charlie said.

'A grand place in Scotland. Badger Burnhard has several properties up there, so I understand.'

Charlie rolled his eyes to the heavens as if he couldn't believe the ridiculousness of what he was hearing. 'Right, so what do we need to do, weasel? Where does Mr Horace Fox need to go to claim his very swish den?'

The weasel mentioned the lovely riverside town of Twickenham, halfway between Richmond and Hampton Court. 'Twickers, the locals call it. That's where you need to go,' he said. 'It's not far.'

'How far exactly?' Charlie said.

'Ooh, say ten miles or so upriver. There's a large house there that's like a creamy-coloured castle. It's called Strawberry Hill House and somewhere in the grounds you'll find the place that now belongs to Mr Horace Fox – if Mr Horace Fox can get there in time to lay claim to what should be his, that is. Five days you've got. You have to get there in the magic hour before close of business at sunrise on Friday.'

The magic hour . . . Horace knew exactly what the weasel meant. *It's that golden time before sunrise when most sticks are asleep and the world belongs to us foxes.*

He thought back to how he used to play out on the scrubland with his brothers and sisters in the early morning light before Ma called them all in for bed.

Five

Beneath the neon light of the Panda Garden Chinese Takeaway, Horace's tail dropped low and he wailed, 'It's too much.' There was the loss of the father he could barely remember, the tragic end of his dear brothers, Eddie and

George, and now there was a price on his head. No legacy could be worth all this pain.

Badger Burnhard was willing to do anything to get the den that should be his and had sent Zigzag McVitie, the deadly hit-snake, after him. Horace knew he needed to run, but all he could do was sit amongst the plastic takeaway cartons with his tail dipped as low as it would go.

'I'm sorry to hear of your loss,' Charlie said, 'but you know your brothers and your pops – they wouldn't want to see you like this. They'd want you to fight on and claim what's yours.'

'But I no longer care about the den. What use is it without my family?'

'Come on, mate, that's no way to talk. You can't let that greedy badger win! That's not what your brothers would want. You've got to pull yourself together and get out there and fight for what is rightfully yours.'

'I know you're right, but it's so hard – too hard.'

Charlie looked at the weasel. 'I might just let you go now.'

'Oh, thank heavens!' the weasel said, clutching his throat.

'All right, Le Hoop, there's one last thing I need to know,' Charlie said.

'Oh yes, yes, sir, anything, sir, anything you need to know, just ask.'

'The snake, this *Zigzag McVitie*, where is he and what does he know?'

Weasel Le Hoop stared fearfully around, and Horace and Charlie looked with him. The yard was clear but dark and dirty with boxes, chicken bones, spare ribs and other debris.

Weasel Le Hoop dropped his voice to a whisper. 'Zigzag McVitie is on your trail. He's set his heart on that posh place in Scotland, and it'll all be his if he kills Horace before the week is out.'

Horace gasped and a shiver ran down his spine.

'Tell me something I don't know,' Charlie said. 'This snake – how close is he?'

'I don't know,' said Weasel Le Hoop. 'I move faster than him and that's how I found you first. You don't see Zigzag McVitie before he attacks. He's onto you, behind you, ready to strike long before you realise.'

'So what's in it for you?' Charlie said. 'Why were you hired?'

'I'm a detective, award-winning – you must have heard of me, surely?'

Horace shrugged and Charlie shook his head. 'Nope, never heard of you.'

'I have an excellent reputation with many happy customers who'll all put in a good word for me. Go ahead and ask anyone.'

'Get to the point, weasel,' Charlie said.

'Badger Burnhard hired me to find Mr Horace Fox, that's all. I'm not violent by nature. My job is done.'

'Hmm, so you'll be reporting back, no doubt.' Charlie frowned. 'Horace, grab Mr Le Hoop for me.'

Horace did as Charlie asked, though he wasn't too sure of himself with his young jaws gripped around Weasel Le Hoop's fidgeting neck.

Am I doing this right?

He'd never held a creature this big before.

Charlie, ears pricked, looked carefully around the yard before fastening his jaws firmly back around the weasel.

'Please, I beg you, leave me be!'

But Charlie had other ideas and carried Le Hoop to the top of a wall.

The weasel wriggled and kicked. 'Let me go, I beg of you,' he pleaded.

But Charlie took a step back and then with one almighty thrust, chucked Le Hoop into a large black recycling bin.

'*Help!*' squealed Weasel Le Hoop as he flew through the air.

There was a moment's silence, followed by a small *thwack!* as Le Hoop landed.

'Didn't sound too bad,' Charlie said. 'He'll survive.'

'Hey, let me out!' Le Hoop's voice was muffled. 'Get me out of here. I won't tell anyone where you are. I'll say you got away. Trust me, please – get me out.'

'Too bad, Le Hoop – trusting you is not something we can do,' Charlie said. 'Just be grateful we won't tell the sticks or you'll be stir-fry.'

The foxes left the yard laughing, but their cheerful mood didn't last long.

'Zigzag McVitie could be anywhere,' Charlie said.

Horace gulped. 'We need to be on our guard. I say we try that direction.'

'How about hiding on a train and getting away?' Charlie said. 'There must be one that goes that way. It would speed everything up. We'd be there in no time.'

Horace's eyes filled with tears as he struggled to say two words: 'Uncle Henry'.

'Oh sorry, mate, forgive me. I clean forgot. No trains ever, I promise.'

'No trains, no tracks,' Horace said.

Charlie nodded. 'There's only one thing us foxes can rely on – or rather four things – and that's our legs, our four legs, and that's what matters. That, and what we hear, smell and see.' But Horace wasn't listening. 'What are you looking at?'

'Check out that sign.'

Hanging from an old black and white, wood-framed building was a painted sign of a fox and a castle.

'Well, I never. Would you look at that – a fox and a castle. Who'd have thought it?' Charlie shook his head. 'All of a sudden I feel a whole lot better about this. Let's get off to

Twickenham so you can claim what's rightfully yours.'

'Yes, let's get going – but which way?'

Charlie shrugged. Neither fox had a clue so they sniffed the air. The scent of the river was on the wind so they knew it wasn't far.

Skulking in the shadows, they followed the pavement and then made a run for it across a road, before nipping down an alleyway and around the back of some large buildings, crossing a cobbled walkway and finally arriving at the riverside. The dark river shone below them with the reflection of lights from the grand buildings on either side. In the distance sat a large egg-shaped dome in front of gleaming tower blocks.

'What a view! This is my town,' Charlie said. 'I love this city.'

Horace meanwhile had found a sausage which he wolfed down in one go. He coughed and spluttered and his eyes began to water.

'You having some kind of fit?' Charlie said. 'Shush! You're attracting too much attention. Shut up, will you!' Charlie shunted Horace down some steps to an icy puddle. 'Drink, you fool. What's the matter with you?'

'There was this sausage or rather half a sausage and I gobbled it up, but then the coughing began and I couldn't stop.'

Charlie rolled his eyes. 'Did this sausage have yellow sauce by any chance?'

'Yes, yes, it did. How did you know?'

'Mustard – you've eaten a hot dog with hot mustard, you idiot.'

Horace felt himself redden beneath his shiny orangey-red fur.

'Check with me next time you come across some new food you don't know. Mustard is maybe not for youngsters like you.' Charlie shook his head. 'I don't know – the youth of today, completely clueless.'

Horace pulled a face and stuck out his tongue.

'What's the matter now?'

'It's that puddle – it tastes horrible.'

With a sigh, Charlie dipped his tongue in the small pool of water. 'It's salty – must be from the river when the tide's been in. Come on.'

'Which way?'

'Now you've got me.'

The foxes looked in both directions and agreed that the river looked the same both ways. They really didn't have a clue which direction to set off in.

'Upriver has to be the opposite from downriver,' Horace said.

'Right,' Charlie said.

'So if we see how the water flows, then we go the opposite way.'

The foxes took their time and watched the dark water ripple and flow in one clear direction.

'Other way then,' Charlie said.

Horace smiled. 'Let's go and claim my den.'

'The castle of dens,' Charlie said.

'A den so fantastic Badger Burnhard will do anything to get his filthy, thieving, property-grabbing paws on it.'

'Don't think about him,' Charlie said.

'It's hard not to,' Horace said, 'but we'll show him.'

Six

The riverside was lit by fancy black lamps with a big coiled fish at their base. Seeing seafood made Horace's tummy groan.

'Blimey, is that you? You've only just eaten!' Charlie said.

'I told you, I'm a growing fox.'

'You'll be growing outwards if you carry on like that!'

The foxes stopped to check both sides of the river. There were no cars on the other side.

'It's quieter over there,' Horace said. 'We should cross.'

They looked towards a silver bridge shining over the dark water.

'Let's go!' Charlie said.

The foxes jogged up the steps to make their way across but there were too many sticks and the foxes had to dodge their way through as best they could.

On the other side, reflections from the lamps rippled out over the dark water like a stream of jewels. Sticks in couples and groups spilled out of the restaurants and bars all along the bank.

'Quick, over here!' Charlie dashed out of sight into the

shadows and they made a run for it through subways and along walkways. They sprinted under bridges, past a ship docked at a riverside mooring, past markets and a glass building shaped like a gleaming giant onion. Tired, they slowed a little but began to notice more.

Horace paused. 'Look over there.' He nodded over to the other side of the river where a grey castle with four towers sat inside a high wall. 'Could that be Strawberry Hill House? The weasel said it was a castle.'

'I'll ask someone – maybe it is your castle.' Charlie looked around but the streets were empty. There was a strange eerie silence.

Ahead stood a bridge with a square tower at either end.

'Let's cross and see,' Horace said.

The foxes climbed the steps onto the bridge where heavy traffic blasted fumes at fox-level. Coughing, they scurried across.

The castle's pale perfect walls were high and its gate was firmly shut.

'Round here.' Horace had spotted a wooden bridge leading to a small courtyard. Charlie ran ahead and jumped from a bench to a ridge so he could scramble up the wall and peek inside. Horace followed.

'There's a bird,' Charlie said. 'Looks like an overgrown blackbird. Excuse me,' he asked politely, 'is this Strawberry Hill House?'

The large tar-black bird opened one eye and looked down her beak at the foxes. 'You are absurd.' She closed her eye and turned her head.

Charlie looked like he was about to have a go, but Horace stopped him. 'Hello, I wonder if you could help,' Horace said, 'only we're looking for Strawberry Hill House. We're told it's a castle and, well, this is certainly a castle. And you look like someone who knows what's what.'

The bird reopened her eye and looked Horace up and down. 'I can tell *you* what's what – you are both stupid and absurd.'

'There's no need to be rude,' Horace said. 'Are you a crow?

The bird looked skywards as if she thought Horace a complete idiot. 'I am a raven and this is the Tower of London where traitors are sent to while away their final days before they are beheaded or hanged. There is nothing strawberry about this place, apart from the colour of the traitors' spilt blood.'

Horace pulled a face. 'Oh right, I'm so glad I asked. Do you know where we can find Strawberry Hill House?'

'Never heard of it.' She turned her back on the foxes.

Charlie shrugged. 'Forget it. We're wasting time.'

They stayed on that side of the river. It didn't seem worth crossing back when they didn't know which side Strawberry Hill House stood on.

Sticking as close to the river as they could, they ran past tower blocks, down walkways, over benches, round roundabouts and past warehouses.

The sky was black and it was icy cold.

Ducking into a small park, they found a large beech tree with bark chips at the foot of it where the snow had melted. Horace flopped to the ground and rolled in it.

'The bark's so soft,' he said. 'It reminds me of home.'

'Get up, you loon. We need to get on.'

Horace sat up and immediately slumped back down. 'I'm so tired and exhausted. Surely we've done ten miles already but there's no sign of my castle. Maybe the whole thing is a lie – one big fat weaselly fib.'

'No one would send Zigzag McVitie unless there was something worth having. We can't let you lose out to that greedy Badger Burnhard. Come on, we must be nearly there.'

Horace shivered. 'Those names – McVitie and Burnhard – they give me the heebie-jeebies.'

Charlie jumped into the air and pounced down. 'Gotcha!' he said, holding a rat up by its tail.

'Ah look, leave it out, fox. I've had it up to here with you lot!' The rat's solid body swung from side to side as it hung from Charlie's mouth. 'Honestly, it's just bullying and there ain't no excuse. I mean there's so much grub left out round here. You don't need to catch anything live and breathing, know what I mean?'

Charlie opened his mouth to let the rat go but then stamped on its tail before it could run off. 'You don't look too tasty but you *can* and *will* talk to me.'

The rat sighed. He was a fat rat with scabby skin and flaky fur – not too pretty. 'What's the matter, fox, you lonely or something? Need someone to talk to?'

Charlie laughed. 'Handsome fox like me? Do me a favour.'

The rat shrugged. 'You get all sorts round here.'

Horace stepped forward. 'Where are we exactly?'

'You don't know where you are?' The rat looked surprised. 'That's basic knowledge, that is. That's crucial, like, fundamental. If you don't know where you are, how can you know which way to go?' He curled his lip. 'Isle of Dogs, mate. Not the best address in town they say, but you'll never go hungry here – rubbish dumped everywhere. Bliss it is, food-wise. It's the land of opportunity. Perfect for those with a nose, you get me?'

'Isle of Dogs?' Horace said. 'Are there packs of dogs here?'

'I dunno about packs of dogs,' the rat said, 'but there are certainly a few pooches hanging about, though they usually have sticks in tow which must be a dreadful bind in my honest opinion.'

Horace glanced around. 'Have you heard of a place called Strawberry Hill House?'

The rat looked away for a moment as if searching deep in the darkest corners of his small ratty brain. He shook his head. 'Nah, Canary Wharf maybe or Silvertown and then there's the Gherkin – that funny-looking building over there – but no Strawberry House, no, never heard of it.'

'How far is Twickenham from here?' Charlie said.

'I don't know nothing about no Twickenham.'

'Is this upriver or downriver?' Horace asked.

'Oh, bless my shish kebab, how would I know? Best you ask some river types. There are water voles down there and herons and gulls, if they'll talk to you. Foxes ain't flavour of the month round here though. It's all that stashing and storing of extra food you do – it annoys folk, know what I mean?'

Horace slumped; his ears were down and his tail was low. 'We're nowhere near Twickenham, are we?' He looked down towards the dark river. 'We've gone the wrong way, I know it.'

Seven

To find out where they were, the foxes went back to the river, where a gull hovered in the air, low over the brown water.

'Hey you!' Charlie shouted.

The gull screeched. 'Whatever it is, I'm not interested.'

'How rude,' Horace said, but Charlie had other things on his mind. He'd caught sight of a slight movement in the mud. 'What is it?' Horace strained to see, as Charlie darted sideways and then pounced on a small furry creature the colour of ditchwater.

There was a squeal as Charlie got it by the leg.

'Help! Let me go, you brute.'

He'd caught a water vole, and almost at once her mate and their babies all came peeking out from their muddy hole. 'Let go! Leave her alone.'

'We mean you no harm,' Horace said. 'We just have a few questions for you.'

'Let go of her then and we'll talk.'

Horace nodded at Charlie and against his will, he released his catch, who immediately scurried back to her family.

'We need to know about the river,' Horace said. 'We thought we were travelling upstream but now we're not so sure.'

The male water vole nodded. 'It's a common mistake,' he said. 'This stretch of the Thames follows the tides in and out from the sea, so water can move one way and then turn around and go the other way, just like that, ebb and flow, two high tides a day. It can be confusing for those who don't know.'

Horace's fears were right – they'd gone many miles in the wrong direction. Both foxes realised at the same time and they slumped down, their tails drooping.

'We've gone downstream by mistake, haven't we?' Horace said.

The water voles nodded.

'How far are we from Central Stickland?'

'We wouldn't know. We've never been,' the female water vole said.

'I'm told it's around ten miles,' the male water vole said.

Horace stared down at his paws. 'So it's ten miles back to where we started and then another ten to Twickenham? I don't think I can do that right now.'

Charlie nodded. 'Where can we rest up round here?'

'There's a tunnel,' the male water vole said. 'It takes you under the river and you'll find a large park on the other side. I've heard it's fancy – the perfect place to bed down for the day.'

The sun was rising, bedtime for foxes, so they left the water voles and ran through the damp tiled tunnel which took them under the river. At the other end, they leapt up the steps into sunlight.

Charlie squinted. 'That sun will melt all the snow.'

Horace stopped at a bin and pulled out a tray of cold chips, scarlet with ketchup, and some curling ham sandwiches which he shared with Charlie.

After their nosh-up, they ran through several busy streets until they located the park. Horace chose a clump of three fat bushes that would shield them from view and they curled up close together for warmth.

'Dare we sleep?' Horace said.

'There is no way Zigzag McVitie will be looking for us in the Isle of Dogs or wherever we are, ten miles or so in the wrong direction,' Charlie said. 'My guess is he's halfway to Twickenham, wondering why he can't find us. I hear what you're saying though, so we'll take it in turns, one on lookout, one having a snooze.'

A rotten eggy pong suddenly filled the undergrowth.

'Oh Charlie, did you have to?'

'Sorry, mate, must be all those takeaways.'

Horace smiled. 'I know – Boom by name, boom by nature.'

And with that, young Horace dozed off while Charlie kept watch, his ears, nose, eyes and whiskers on full alert for the slightest creep or slither from that dreaded snake. They then swapped over and Charlie rested while Horace acted as lookout. But even though Horace was fearful and wanted to do his best, his eyelids soon grew heavy until his head dipped and they both slept through until dusk.

On waking, they found the snow had melted to slush and they were happy to see the green of the grass once again and to feel the earth slightly warmer beneath their paws.

Thirsty, they visited a half-frozen lake and gulped at the icy water.

'We need to make up for lost time,' Charlie said.

Horace shook the water from his face. 'So which way, boss?'

The foxes left the park, determined not to make any more mistakes.

'Let's go back to the river,' Charlie said. 'That way we can get our bearings and make sure we head in the right direction.'

'It's definitely left.' Horace could see a large squat dome-shaped building to his right, while across the river gleamed shiny office blocks, brightly lit in the fading light. 'That's where we were yesterday.' With his nose he pointed across the river. 'That's the park where you caught the rat.'

Charlie nodded. 'We can stay on this side, as long as we go left and keep going left.'

The foxes looked down at the brown water. The river was now flowing in the opposite direction from the previous day. Horace shook his head. 'Fancy getting it so wrong. What a doofus you are.'

'Sort it out, it was your fault.'

'No way, I said go the other way.'

'No, you didn't, I said go left.'

'You didn't.'

'I did.'

'Didn't.'

'Did.'

Laughing, they ran along the riverside past a ship in dry dock and then down a busy road, before moving back to the river's edge. Dashing past wharfs and docks, the foxes trusted the river to show them the way.

'I could do with some brekkie,' Horace said. It was getting on for late evening and foxes like their breakfast long before then.

'All right, Hungry Horace, I hear you.' Charlie's smile quickly faded. 'It's awfully quiet.'

'Yes, I thought that.'

They trotted on with ears pricked as they scanned the path ahead.

'There are no sticks anywhere,' Horace said.

The docks were empty, and so were the offices.

'I don't like it. Stickland's never this quiet. Something ain't right,' Charlie said. 'Mind you, there's no point in worrying about it, not with that snake on our case.'

On and on they ran through street after street, where again

all the shops, cafés and restaurants were either closed or boarded up: Athena Kebabs – shut; Planet Pizza – shut; Zam Zam Supermarket – shut. There was no pizza, no kebabs, no fried chicken, no fish and chips. It was all really strange and it was the same wherever they went.

'What on earth is going on?' Charlie said.

They checked the bins – every bin they came across. 'Here's one.' Horace took a running jump, dived in, nose to the bottom, searching for scraps of anything vaguely tasty. 'Nothing, not a bean.'

'Empty, all empty,' Charlie said. 'I reckon someone or something has been here before us. I don't know. We'll have to kill something.'

'Can you remember how?'

Charlie looked around, his ears pricked and nose up.

There was a grey one-legged pigeon perched high on a wall.

'You'll never get that,' Horace said. 'Not unless it falls off.'

'Let's move on.' Charlie led the way along slush-covered pavements, past more closed shops and takeaways. They were back at the big bridge now and could see the Tower of London across the river.

'Shall we eat that horrible raven?' Horace said.

Charlie laughed. 'Nothing would give me more pleasure than to silence that stuck-up bird, but the walls are too high. Let's try down here.'

There was a small city park, a patch of green land squeezed in between the river and the shops and offices.

Nose to the ground, Charlie cased the joint, checking behind benches, in bushes and at the base of a holly tree where he pulled out a few skinny worms, while Horace found some beetles.

'Bit chewy,' Charlie said.

'Too crunchy.' Horace made a face. 'You know, I'm not so

keen on bugs these days, not since being in the city with all its food from around the world.' He'd become choosy about what he ate just like Charlie and all the other city foxes. But even the fussiest eater can be too hungry to care. Horace spotted a dead mouse on the path – small, grey and shrivelled. He ate half and passed the rest to his friend.

'It's going to be a long hard day walking on so little food,' Charlie said.

A seagull, high up on a post, looked down its beak and screeched with laughter.

'Get lost!' Charlie said. 'I hate those birds.'

From here on, they were back in familiar surroundings. It was where they'd been the day before. The foxes went back the way they had come, passing glass buildings, a ship in dry dock, a theatre, an art gallery and other grand buildings.

It was a while since they'd seen any sticks but suddenly they could see a big gathering up ahead. As the foxes drew closer, they could see that these sticks were huddled around a van, while other sticks handed out soup and bread.

'Happy Christmas, Bill,' a stick said as he dished out the soup.

The foxes hid behind a concrete column and watched in the hope there'd be scraps, but had no luck.

Horace and Charlie continued on past young sticks who were whizzing around on skateboards and past a huge silver Ferris wheel. Their ears were pricked and on full alert.

Charlie looked nervous. 'Did you hear that?'

'No.'

'Exactly.'

'What does that mean?'

'McVitie.'

'McVitie?'

'He's on to us.'

'How do you know?'

'I can just sense it, that's all.'

A sick feeling rose in Horace's throat and he struggled to speak. 'You're never wrong, are you? What if he gets me?'

'He'll be snake stew before he gets anywhere near you.' Charlie sounded as confident as always, though he kept checking behind. 'I think it's best we change tack and do a little zigzagging of our own, back and forth over the river to get him confused. We'll cross at the next bridge.'

The foxes trotted on and soon reached a wide stone bridge. Horace ran ahead up the steps. 'I love steps!' He leapt to the top and then stopped. 'What's that?' His fur bristled as he stared at a large fancy tower at the other end of the bridge.

'What's what?' Charlie said.

'That ... that tower with the huge white eye looking down.'

'It's a clock.'

Horace trembled. 'It's like a giant eye!'

'It's just a clock – nothing to worry about.'

'But it's not just a clock, is it?'

'You've lost me, mate – what are you on about?'

'It feels like Badger Burnhard is watching me, watching my every move, ready to send in the snake to bump me off.'

'Horace, you're losing the plot, mate. It's just a clock. Get a grip!'

'But time is running out. That's what the clock is telling me.' And at that very moment the giant clock bonged its deep heavy chime, announcing the top of the hour.

In their rush, the foxes dashed over the bridge, past Big Ben and the Houses of Parliament and on to a large square with grand stone buildings on all sides and a grassed area in the middle with statues of famous sticks.

Taking a left, they ran through a small riverside park and along a main road, past a handsome white building with elegant columns and then a smart block of flats. Horace peeked in the windows, longing to see the warm glow of home. It reminded him of his own snug ditch on the scrubland by the railway track with his sisters and Ma.

Next came a bridge all decked out in white lights, houseboats, a power station and shops selling strange old things. Horace would have liked to linger, but there wasn't time. Turning left, they moved on to a quieter area with rows of little houses and then after running on for a good mile or so, they reached a huge complex of flats at the end of the road.

'We'll run through,' Charlie said. There was a walkway and as always the foxes wanted to take the quickest route.

The flats were modern and high-rise, with smart-looking shops and restaurants at ground level. As they ran through, they could see a harbour with boats.

'We're back at the river.' Charlie bombed along the metal walkway but it curved around, taking them past the boats and back away from the river.

'I don't get it?' Horace said.

'There's no access,' Charlie said.

'What now?'

'About turn,' Charlie said, and they ran back the other way, past the shops and restaurants and away from the smart flats, where they took a left and followed the road, across a roundabout and under a railway bridge.

They reached a street of terraced houses and through the windows Horace could see sticks eating huge heaped platefuls of food. His stomach rumbled.

'All that food – it's so unfair,' Horace said.

A few doors down, a stick came out of a house holding a bulging black sack which he placed in a bin before going back inside.

'It smells meaty!' Horace's nose was up and his tongue was dripping so they entered the front garden and went up to the bin.

Charlie shook his head. 'These plastic bins are impossible,' he said.

'Can we knock it over?'

They took a run at it and shoved as hard as they could, but the bin just scraped a fraction along the ground.

'Forget it,' Charlie said. 'We'll have to keep going.'

Horace sighed. His stomach hurt. 'Sometimes it's tough being a fox.'

They both knew only too well that they had small stomachs that needed to be regularly supplied with meals. Like all foxes, they were unable to store fat like big greedy animals such as badgers.

All of a sudden, Horace leapt back, baring his teeth.

'What is it?' Charlie said.

'I heard a hiss and thought it was Zigzag McVitie.' Horace nodded towards a tabby on the fence, its back arched, fur on end.

The cat hissed, 'Back off, buster! This is my territory.'

'Chill, we're not interested,' Charlie said.

The foxes left, ears pricked, noses down, sniffing the ground and the air all around as they headed into a deserted supermarket car park. The place was shut and the bins were empty. There was nothing to be had here either.

Back on the main road, there were more flats – a tall block this time. Following the whiff of meat, they found a bin area where someone had left a black sack on the ground.

'This is it,' Horace said. 'This is what I've been waiting for – a black sack stuffed with food.' They ripped into it, sending plastic wrappers flying, as they located a turkey carcass. Within seconds, they had stripped it down to clean bare bones.

Horace licked the grease from his lips and cheeks.

Charlie smiled. 'It seems all the sticks are at home feasting.

Maybe they'll be chucking out plenty over the next few days and we'll soon have more food than we can eat.'

Continuing on their way, they came to a busy road where they listened hard, their hearing far better than their sight.

'Why is it always so hard to judge?' Horace said.

They listened. They looked. There was a small gap or so they thought. They shot across. A motorbike swerved and a car honked its horn.

'Only just made it.' Horace's heart was thumping as they ran at full pelt.

'That was close.' Charlie's eyes were wide. 'Let's head that way.' He nodded to the left and once again they returned to the water's edge where they'd have the river to guide them. Wharf after wharf, a dock and then through a park with tennis courts, a swimming pool and a croquet lawn.

'This is more like it!' Horace slowed his pace so he could take in the surroundings. 'It's lovely here – relaxing.'

'Are you crazy? We need to keep going. We have to get to Twickenham to claim your den on time. I don't want Badger Burnhard getting his filthy claws on what is rightfully yours. And then there's McVitie to consider. He could be anywhere.'

'Aargh!' Horace yelped suddenly. 'Get off me!' He'd been caught from behind. He tried to flip around, baring his teeth, but it was no good. One fox had his neck and another had caught a leg, while two more leapt on Charlie.

'Let go! Get off me,' Horace shouted.

'Easy,' Charlie said, doing his best to shrug them off.

Horace and Charlie were pulled across the park to the back of a whitewashed clapboard building, where a slim red fox with a thick blood-orange tail sat on the top step.

'So what do we have here?' the slim fox said. 'Delinquents?'

'What does that mean?' Horace asked.

'Criminals, bad news, troublemakers.'

'I'd say you lot seem to be the troublemakers round here,' Charlie said, 'Who are you anyway?'

'Who are *you*? And what are you both doing, trespassing on the land of his Grace, his Excellency, the Bishop?'

Charlie's mouth fell open. *'You're the Bishop?'*

The Bishop lifted his thick blood-orange tail. 'I am he.'

'Your Grace.' Charlie bowed, nudging Horace to do the same.

'Shall we try again? Who are you and what is your business here?'

'I'm Charlie Boom and this is Horace Fox. We're on our way to Twickenham.'

'Twickenham? You mean you're headed South of the River?' The Bishop looked appalled.

'Is it far, do you know?' Horace said.

'You cannot go to Twickenham, not without my permission anyhow. I do not let just anyone cross my land. Oh no, imagine that – open doors, chaos it would be. Pandemonium.'

'I'm sorry, your Grace. I didn't know. I'm only young,' Horace said.

'Your friend here, he's not so young. What's his excuse?'

Charlie tensed his jaw. 'We're under a lot of pressure, your Grace. Young Horace here, his life is in danger. Zigzag McVitie is after him and if he doesn't get to Twickenham before the week is out, well, he stands to lose everything that is rightfully his.'

'And what, pray, is "*everything*"?'

'It's a den in the grounds of Strawberry Hill House.'

'Strawberry Hill House? That's a very fine house – a castle even. Isn't that where Loveness Foxduka lives?'

Horace pricked his ears. He had never heard of Loveness Foxduka, but her name alone made her sound quite wonderful. 'Who is Loveness Foxduka?'

'Loveness is a dear young vixen and her mother Claretina is an old friend. I rarely see them now since they moved South of the River.'

Charlie fidgeted, aware of their need to press on. 'So you see, we need to get to Strawberry Hill House as soon as possible.'

The Bishop nodded. 'Otherwise young Horace loses everything? But why?'

'There's a badger, Badger Burnhard, who wants the den – and he'll do anything to get his paws on it.'

'Badger Burnhard?' The Bishop spat out the name. 'That lousy itchy-arsed lump is responsible for so much misery amongst our fox brothers. You should have said. Of course we must help you. Help you we will.'

The Bishop controlled one of the largest territories in southwest Stickland. It stretched all the way from the posh Hurlingham Club to Bishop's Park, the vast grounds of a riverside palace. The Bishop didn't live in the palace itself, but deep amongst the park's thickest bushes. His followers now led the way past large houses and blocks of flats, under the bridge and into Bishop's Park, where they pushed back branches and bushes so that Horace, Charlie and the Bishop could walk through with ease.

In single file, they passed through a walled garden, followed by woodland, a meadow and a knot garden, with clipped box hedges. Finally, there was a wall covered in holly and ivy, below which had been dug a perfect round foxhole.

'After you,' the Bishop said.

Horace jumped into the hole which turned into a long dark tunnel. Inching forward, he was followed by Charlie and the Bishop and then the other foxes. Further on they reached an enormous round den.

A deep and heavy bark sounded in the air.

The Bishop licked his lips. 'Suppertime. Do join us.'

Foxes filed in from tunnels on either side each carrying offerings which they dropped in the middle of the round chamber.

Horace and Charlie stared at the feast of scavenged food with its bones and scraps of turkey, sausages, roast potatoes, crumbling slices of bread and cake, and half-eaten fruit and biscuits. No wonder the bins of central Stickland were empty. The Bishop's army had been there first and taken the lot.

'Tuck in, my friends, tuck in,' the Bishop said.

The foxes fell on the food in their usual frenzy and within seconds everything had gone, leaving not a sausage, chicken leg or crust of bread.

Charlie sat back. 'Thanks ever so, your Grace – that was excellent!'

Horace smiled. 'I can't remember the last time I felt this good.' He was sure he could hear his bones creak as he grew a little. 'You've been most kind, your Grace. We are truly grateful. Now we really ought to get going to Twickenham.'

The Bishop frowned. 'Twickenham, at this time?'

'What time is it?' Charlie said, because it wasn't obvious down in the Bishop's den, which was so dark and cosy that it always seemed like night.

'It's daybreak,' the Bishop said. 'I wouldn't recommend going out now. Sticks are a terrible nuisance round here. And what about this McVitie character?'

Horace felt ill at the mention of Zigzag McVitie and had to sit very still in order to keep his dinner down.

'It's best you travel under cover of darkness,' the Bishop said. 'Stay here and rest and then at dusk, after a hearty breakfast, my Special Endeavours Team will escort you *South of the River*.'

Eight

South of the River was a no-go zone, the badlands of Stickland, according to the Bishop. It was no longer his territory and his power and influence counted for little once he passed over that bridge, so he never went.

Horace and Charlie, however, needed to take the most direct route to Twickenham. At least they had enjoyed a deep sleep in a grand chamber lined with scraps of soft fabric that must have been scavenged from the finest bins of southwest Stickland.

Horace felt so comfortable that he dreamt of home – his dear old Ma, his sisters Kitty and May, and his poor brothers Eddie, George and Bert. He dreamt they were all alive and together again, playing on the scrubland by the railway track as they had done when they were cubs, and when he woke and realised it was only a dream, tears rolled down his cheeks and his tail drooped low.

Hearing Charlie stir, Horace quickly wiped his face with his tail.

Thankfully, breakfast cheered Horace up. It was a wonderful spread of warm roadkill and mixed berries.

Horace licked his mouth and cheeks. 'Is that squirrel? I was only saying the other day that I haven't had squirrel in ages.'

'I just can't pass a tree without checking for squirrel. I'm sure it's the same for you,' the Bishop said, but then his face darkened. 'I have news, by the way. A snake matching Zigzag McVitie's description has been spotted on the eastern edge of my land. My team gave chase, of course, but I'm sorry to say that the snake escaped.'

'He's onto us,' Charlie said.

Horace trembled. 'And he's gaining fast.'

The sun had set on a chilly winter afternoon and with their bellies full, Horace and Charlie decided it was the perfect time to resume their journey.

Horace thanked the Bishop. 'We really appreciate all you've done for us.'

'It's been a great pleasure,' the Bishop said. 'Any time you're passing, do drop in, and we would welcome an invite to Strawberry Hill one of these days when it's officially yours.' The Bishop thought for a moment. 'Oh, wait a minute, that's *South of the River*. I don't do *South of the River*.'

'Is it that bad?' Horace said.

'Well, I do have my team of special highly-trained operatives, I suppose.' The Bishop called in his number two, a large fox with only half a tail, and told him to gather a crack force of his four fiercest foxes to accompany Horace and Charlie safely over Putney Bridge to the other side.

The Bishop's foxes led the way back through the tunnel and out of the hole. Going back the way they had come before, they went through the knot garden, meadow and woodland and then up some stone steps up to the road. All seven foxes, ears pricked, shook with the vibrations from the heavy traffic on the bridge.

The Bishop's Special Endeavours Team read the signals for the best moment to enter the bridge. The Bishop's Number

Two reported back. 'Traffic is heavy and there are multiple sticks. There'll be some trouble at the sight of seven foxes but we shall deal with that. I'll lead from the front, followed by two of my team. When I turn and give the nod, my lead foxes will march ahead and you will follow them. The rest of the team will protect you from the rear. Understood?'

Horace and Charlie nodded. 'Understood.'

Ears pricked and noses on high alert, the leaders looked left, back along the road and then right, towards the bridge.

At last the Bishop's Number Two ordered the advance: 'Forward march!' He leapt out from the safety of the steps onto the pavement at the start of the bridge, followed by two members of his team. After ten or so paces, they turned and gave Horace and Charlie the nod.

Horace gulped as he and Charlie followed, with the other two foxes at the rear.

A stick on the pavement froze, startled at the rare and beautiful sight that is a skulk of foxes.

'Wow!' Other sticks stopped too, their mouths open in amazement.

'Hold your nerve,' said Charlie. 'We're nearly across.'

On the other side of the bridge, they could see a church clock tower, a smart block of flats, traffic lights and a curve of shops. The foxes forged across to the other side and then made a swift right-hand turn down a small slope that ran close to the river by a restaurant.

'Halt!' The Bishop's Number Two stood aside. 'This is as far as we go. Our mission is complete,' he said. 'You're on your own from here on. Good luck!'

The Bishop's Number Two and his Special Endeavours Team nodded at Horace and Charlie and then quickly about-turned to return to the bridge where they beat a safe retreat back to the Bishop's land on the other side.

The sky was dark and the river was high with water

lapping at the edge of the bank.

Charlie frowned. 'The river's rising and if we don't get a move on, we'll be cut off from the path.'

'I'll race you,' Horace said, and they ran as fast as they could, past the restaurant, a pub, a boathouse, six or seven rowing clubs, houses and a park. The path then became more like countryside with thick bushes to the left and trees growing along the water's edge.

Horace looked up. 'This is lovely. I don't know what the Bishop's going on about – South of the River is glorious, a bit wilder and more like home.'

'It depends on what you're used to, I guess,' Charlie said. 'Scrubland's not to everyone's taste.'

Running side by side, they moved apart whenever they had to dodge a puddle.

A duck swam nearby and Charlie licked his lips. 'Ooh, that's so tempting.'

'We haven't the time,' Horace said.

Water splashed up and the puddles overflowed to almost fill the path. It was close to flooding. They ran harder, wanting to get as far as possible before they could go no further.

It was darker away from the streetlights, surrounded by trees and bushes. 'Can you smell that?' Horace said.

'It's smoke,' Charlie said. 'Can you hear sticks?'

'I'm bored,' a stick shouted. 'There's nothing going on, nothing to do.'

Horace tensed. 'Are they *delinquents*?' He remembered the word the Bishop had used to describe young troublemakers.

'It's all *so boring*,' the stick said. 'Something to happen. What shall we *do*?'

Charlie's eyes flashed in panic. '*Hide!*' Charlie said.

Pointing his nose at a patch of dense bushes, Horace said, 'They'll never see us in there.' Jumping in, the foxes hunkered down so that only the reflection from their dark amber eyes could be seen from the path.

The sticks were smoking cigarettes, puffing away and blowing smoke rings in the air until they had coughing fits and sounded ill.

'What about we attack them ducks?' the tall one said.

Horace and Charlie tried hard not to cough as the smoke irritated their throats.

'Why don't we go robbing? That's always a laugh,' the shorter stick said.

'Hold your nerve,' Charlie whispered. But then the foxes smelt *dog*.

Trailing behind the sticks came a mottled brown dog with a wide flat head, square jaw, fat neck, small pointy ears and a stubby tail.

'Those dogs are bad news,' Horace said. 'Just look at the size of those jaws!'

The dog barked gruffly, showing its massive teeth.

'Sit tight,' Charlie said.

'He can smell us,' Horace said.

It was true. The dog, nostrils flared, was already heading in their direction.

The foxes broke cover as first Charlie and then Horace leapt from their hidey-hole back onto the path, and then sprinted as fast as they could, easily racing past the sticks, but the dog turned and ran after them, barking in rage and spraying phlegmy globules of spit.

On the foxes went, heads down as their paws pounded along, until Charlie slowed. He was out of breath and the fat-necked dog was gaining on him. Desperate, Charlie glanced over his shoulder and then leapt into the river while the dog stalled as he looked from one fox to the other, unsure as to which one he should follow.

'*Go on, Cruncher, get him!*' the taller stick shouted.

Knowing he was in real danger, Charlie swam like he'd never swum before, all four legs paddling frantically beneath the surface of the water.

'Find a rock – let's smash him!' the short stick said.

'What a laugh,' the other one said, and within seconds they were lobbing stones and rocks at Charlie as he swam.

Horace looked back.

Come on, Charlie, keep going! You can do it.

The dog, green drool dripping from its jaw, jumped into the water and swam after Charlie.

'*Stupid fox!*' the short stick shouted. 'You won't escape Cruncher.'

'He's gonna get you!' the other one shouted.

Horace raced back along the path to where the sticks were searching for more stones and rocks to throw at Charlie.

Come on, Charlie, swim! You can do it.

A powerful rage was rising up in Horace.

How dare they hurt my friend?

He braced himself, mouth open, fangs out, ready to defend his dearest friend. And as the tallest stick bent over to grab another rock, Horace ran at him and bit his bony butt as hard as he could.

'Aargh!' the stick shouted. 'Yow, that hurt.'

The shorter stick jumped up with a spiky branch in his hand, and came at Horace.

Horace snarled, baring his teeth, his sharp young fangs on full display.

The stick lashed out and hit Horace on the side.

Horace yelped but he wouldn't back down. He ran in hard and low at the stick's legs and got in a firm bite on his skinny tattooed ankle.

'He's got me – get him off!' The stick shook his leg to get rid of Horace while the tallest stick went for Horace with another branch, but Horace was too fast for them. He swerved and slipped between their legs, and then ran for it, back along the river looking for Charlie.

The fat-necked dog was on the bank, spluttering and shaking the water from his mottled coat. He seemed to have given up on Charlie.

Pathetic!

Horace gritted his teeth and ran so fast he was a mere flash of orangey-red.

Feeling a whoosh of air as Horace went by, the dog looked up, but was too slow to do anything about it.

Running on, Horace expected to find Charlie not too far ahead, but whichever way he looked, Charlie was not there.

Where are you, Charlie? What happened? What have they done to you?

Back and forth, Horace pushed his nose into every bush and ditch, in search of his friend.

I don't get it. Where are you, Charlie?

Horace's nose, ears and eyes were on highest alert as he searched hard and wished even harder, but still he could not find his friend.

Gone, he's gone – vanished into thin air. Oh Charlie, no, not you too . . .

Horace's eyes welled up. He'd had so much loss in his young life, first Bert and then his older brothers Eddie and George, and his dad Dickie, and now Charlie too.

Don't let this be true. This can't be true – not Charlie. I don't and won't believe it.

'Where are you, brother?' he called as he continued his search. 'Hang tight, Charlie, I'm coming for you.'

Nine

Using the river as his guide, Horace ran for a good mile or so, sniffing the air, trees and grass, hoping and longing for the smallest sign of which way his friend had gone. *Oh Charlie, where are you?*

Deep in his rumbling gut, Horace had a terrible feeling – something was seriously wrong.

The river had risen so high that water had washed over the bank and pooled onto the path. Exhausted, Horace ran on through the puddles and mud, his paws cold and sore, but still he kept going. He had to. Under a fancy green bridge and past schools and playing fields he ran on until he sensed he'd gone too far.

Surely Charlie would have stopped before now?

But there was no trace of him.

Should I turn back? Maybe I missed something?

Horace thought he must have missed some small hint of Charlie's scent left close to the path, which had been washed away by the river water. Or worse.

What if Charlie has drowned?

Horace couldn't bear to think of that.

No, Charlie's alive – he has to be. I just know it.

Turning back, Horace went back the way he had come, ears pricked, nose to the ground as he searched for Charlie's scent. Looking left and right, he searched for any telltale tuft of orange-red fur on a fence or broken branch and breathed in deeply to pick up the tiniest trace of Charlie's aroma, but all he could smell was dog muck, which made him cough. And yes, there it was – a mustardy splurge of diarrhoea. It was probably from that nasty, good-for-nothing brute of a fat-necked fighting dog.

He stopped short. There they were in front of him again – the two sticks with that stupid dog. He was all muscle, teeth and tiny brain. The sticks had branches and the dog was off the lead.

What now?

Taking a deep breath, Horace revved up and ran at them.

Jeering, the sticks raised their branches ready to whack Horace while the fat-necked dog bared his flinty teeth, but Horace saw it coming. He'd learnt enough from Charlie Boom and his ma to put in a last-minute swerve to the right. Through speed and skill, he avoided getting hit and dodged back the other way between the two sticks and out the other side before the stupid dog even thought to change direction.

Looking to his right, Horace could see trees and hedging. He wanted to jump in there but was stopped by the high wire fence.

Is it a fox-proof fence though?

It certainly looked that way.

I don't want to keep running along the river.

He was heading in the wrong direction and there was no point going all the way to the bridge that led back over to the Bishop's land. Scanning the area, he spotted another path, took a swift right and kept on going, past playing fields to the left and more of that luscious vegetation, safely hemmed in by yet more wire fences.

What is that place in there?

It began to pour with rain – great big splashes of water. Horace needed shelter so he could rest, take stock, and gather his energy. Everything seemed so much harder now he was on his own.

Oh Charlie, where are you? Please be okay. I miss you, brother.

The high fence curved in towards a large entrance.

This must be how the sticks get in, and if sticks can get in, so can a fox.

The place was shut.

Drat!

Horace kept going until he saw a break in the fence next to a pond. Horace wasn't too fond of swimming but he had no choice. Jumping in, he foxy-paddled across, while ducks, moorhens and geese fled in a flappy panic.

Rising cold and wet from the pond, he shook his orange-red fur as dry as he could, though it made little difference in all the heavy rain.

All he could see was pond after pond, filled with birds that were panicking at the sight of him.

'Relax, I'm just looking for my friend. Have you seen him? He looks a bit like me, only bigger and older, and he has a chipped tooth. His name's Charlie Boom.'

Ducks, moorhens, geese and a heron stared back, ready to make a dash for it at the first sign of danger.

A goose looked down and said, 'Don't listen to a word he says.'

'What is this place?' Horace said.

'The Wetlands. It's exclusive – by which I mean exclusively for *us*,' the goose said. 'You and your kind are *not* welcome here.'

'Tell me something I don't know.' Horace sat down, his shoulders slumped, his ears drooping and his tail low. The heavy rain was soaking through his coat, making him shiver.

This certainly is the Wetlands all right.

His stomach rumbled.

Not now – be quiet! I've no time for food.

Pacing the paths between the ponds, he called out, '*Charlie! Charlie, are you there?*' Pushing his nose into bushes and between clumps of grass, he sent birds, water voles, and mice fleeing at the sight of him. 'Don't worry, I'm not here to hurt you,' he said over and over, and even though his belly ached and continued to rumble, he had no appetite. Charlie had become everything to him – father, brother and friend all rolled into one.

This is no fun, no fun at all. Who wants to be all alone in a world in which every other creature fears or despises you?

Horace made his way around the largest of the lakes and pushed back the reeds in case Charlie had collapsed there.

Startled at the sight of Horace, a toad inflated its spotted brown throat.

'Steady on!' Horace backed up, repulsed by the toad's slimy bulbous ugliness. 'I'm looking for my friend. Have you seen him?'

Was the toad pulling a face or did he always look that bad? Opening his down-turned mouth, he croaked, 'What does this friend look like?'

'He's bigger than me,' Horace said. 'He's fully grown with a thick coat and a brilliant bushy tail. Oh, and he has one chipped tooth.'

The toad shook his head. 'We don't often get your sort in here and when we do, they get caught in traps or shot.'

Horace tensed and his heart pounded in fear.

'The geese will have alerted security by now.'

'What is this place, the Wetlands?'

'It's a nature reserve and we're protected because we're special.'

'I'm nature too, so what about me – am I not special?'

'Ah, well you see, the trouble is that your kind just can't help how you are. We're given food here, but even if you were provided with lots of it, you'd still kill if you could.'

'That's unfair – I haven't done that in ages. These days I prefer to eat my way around the world, thanks to the excellent takeaways in this fine city.' Horace's mouth was watering but he shook his head – he was far too upset to eat. 'So they set traps and shoot foxes here?'

'Yep – expect to get caged or shot. Any minute now a gun will go off and you'll be blasted up the jacksie.'

'The *what?*'

'You know, the jacksie – your backside.'

Horace's stomach twisted. 'So how do I get out of here?'

'The same way you got in, I would suggest.'

Horace turned.

Which way? Which way?

In his panic to escape he became confused.

I don't know which way – help!

He ran around aimlessly and ended up circling several ponds before finding the one he needed to swim across. Jumping into the icy water, he suddenly found himself mobbed by a whole bunch of swans, Canada geese, ducks, coots, moorhens and cormorants.

'Oi, stop bullying, will you! I'm going.' Horace tried to swim faster but his foxy-paddle just wasn't up to it. With his paws stabbing at the water, he battled on as the honking geese pecked at his neck and ears.

'Leave off – get away!' Horace turned his head to snap at them, but as he did so, he caught a glimpse of something black and white in the bushes on the bank.

His heart beat ten times faster and then some.

Something evil was slithering in the long grass, he was sure of it, and Horace was well aware there could only be one explanation.

It's a snake – the snake – Zigzag McVitie – the hit-snake that's been sent to get me!

Horace's own eyes, his off-the-scale heartbeat and jangling nerves were enough for him to know it was real.

I know what I just saw – it's him!

Meanwhile the bird squad continued their mobbing as Horace paddled frantically through the cold pond water and scrabbled up the opposite bank, his paws sinking into the mud as the geese honked and snapped at him, tearing fur from his retreating backside.

'Get off me!' Short of breath and his eyes bulging, Horace's head felt so hot, he thought he'd explode. 'Get off and leave me be!' He leapt out onto the opposite bank while the birds hissed, quacked and flapped, laughing at having seen off the young fox.

'You're only birds – get over yourselves!' he said. 'It's the snake I'm worried about . . .'

He couldn't let them bother him, not when there was Zigzag McVitie on his case, somewhere close and gaining on him fast.

Where are you, Charlie? Please help me, someone – anyone. Help!

Ten

Head down and ears back, Horace was determined to leave the snake far behind as he sprinted back to the river.

Sniffing the air, he smelt river water to the left and the path looked familiar. Yes, he could smell his own scent where he'd left his mark hours before. It was the path he'd escaped down when he'd last seen the sticks with the fat-necked dog. He'd run back that way, get his bearings and move on.

Just as he had thought, he was back at the riverside where the fight had taken place earlier – the very spot where he had last seen Charlie.

It was nearly dawn now. He needed food and somewhere safe to shelter during the daylight hours. He ran on past blocks of smart riverside flats.

'Charlie, Charlie?' He listened hard and sniffed the air.

Food!

He followed the smell through a low hole in a fence and ran across a lawn, triggering a security light.

Ah . . .

He froze, caught in the middle of a bright pool of light. The windows of the house were still dark. Creeping around the outside of the building, Horace followed his nose all the way to a silver metal dish filled with meaty chunks in jelly.

Oh my days, look at that grub! That's what Charlie would say.

Horace hoped that the more he kept Charlie alive in his thoughts, the more he could somehow help Charlie's chances of survival.

I just know he's going to walk round the next corner like nothing ever happened?

It was hard to think anything else of a fox so full of life as his friend Charlie.

Horace checked the area. This food didn't appear to belong to anyone. It was up for grabs, he was sure of it. Sticking his snout straight in, he wolfed down the meat and licked the bowl clean.

If you like something, eat it all.

Looking up, he saw a small metal box pointing down at the dish; it moved slightly every time Horace moved.

The darkness was lifting now and the sun was almost up. Horace needed to take cover and rest. He looked around, checking for snakes.

Everything seemed perfectly still and quiet.

Running around the edge of the garden, Horace searched for somewhere safe to lay his head.

Next to the hedge in the far end corner, he found a compost heap – a tall, dark green mound of decaying grass, cuttings and kitchen scraps. It smelt damp and warm and was most likely full of juicy worms. He burrowed in, making himself a bed towards the back.

Charlie?

Horace found the faintest whiff of his friend's distinctive smell. He sniffed around frantically but the scent marking didn't go anywhere. Tired and confused, he tossed and turned, sending grass cuttings up into the air as he struggled to sleep.

Where are you, Charlie? Please be okay.
How much further to go now?
Where is Twickenham?
Will I make it in time? I can't do this on my own.

Fretting but exhausted, he finally fell asleep.

It was late afternoon as the winter sun bowed out and Horace opened his eyes in the warmth of the grassy heap.

I can do this!

I must do this. I will do this.

I'll do it for Charlie.

The sleep had revived him.

A door opened at the back of the house and an old stick in a long tartan dressing gown came out, carrying the silver bowl that Horace had eaten from earlier.

As before, it smelt of meaty chunks with jelly. Horace's stomach rumbled. He forced himself to stay put until the stick had gone back indoors, then leapt out of the compost heap, throwing grass cuttings and slugs up into the air, and ate so furiously that the bowl made scraping noises on the hard surface of the patio. Looking up, he saw two old sticks watching at the window.

Horace backed away from the bowl. He'd finished anyway.

They would watch him leave, he knew that, but he didn't feel threatened. He sensed they liked him. Ma had said that some sticks love foxes.

Heading off across the lawn, he tripped the security light and once again was in the spotlight. He paused and looked back.

The stick in the tartan gown put her hands to her face, while the other one smiled.

Grateful for the free meal they had provided, Horace waved his tail in thanks and set back across the garden to the hole in the fence and out again to the riverside. He was feeling a whole lot more ready to continue on his way to Twickenham, hoping he'd find Charlie and at the same time give the snake the slip and claim the den his father had left him.

Eleven

The river had dropped so low while Horace slept that only a trickle of water was flowing down the middle. Horace held his breath as he scanned the mud, terrified he might see Charlie's body, bedraggled and lifeless.

There was an old street sign, a deflated football, some rotting branches and a plank of wood, a sunken boat, a bicycle frame and a shopping trolley, but no Charlie.

Horace was back at the fancy green bridge now. Running underneath, he followed the path past floodlit playing fields, tennis courts and a couple of large buildings, before reaching a tangle of trees and bushes.

'*Charlie!*' Horace called out every few paces. 'Charlie, are you there?'

He tried to search every bush, every briar, every overgrown ditch, but was up against it. Charlie could be anywhere and time was running out. Moving on with his ears pricked and his nose on high alert, he searched as best he could for the faintest trace of his friend.

The wilderness soon gave way to housing that curved away from the river, making way for buildings along the edge of the river. Jumping over a picnic table, Horace balanced along a wall and then returned to the towpath. After passing a restaurant, some offices, a brewery and then going under another bridge, he slowed to peek through a hole in the wall. On the other side, he saw bouquets of flowers on the ground and some helium balloons and a teddy bear sitting on a mound of fresh grass. The sky was a deep blue, cloudless with stars and a full moon, while the bare branches of the trees, black against the sky, swayed in the wind as if waving a warning.

A crackle sounded somewhere close behind.

Horace jumped.

What was that?

He froze, his ears pricked.

Silence.

Creeping on, he stepped along cautiously, listening hard to the sounds on the night air.

Hey, what's that?

Something was above him.

It was a bat flying low, almost skimming the fur on his head.

There was a rustle of leaves and he spun round.

White? Did I see white?

He thought he'd caught sight of a bright flash moving amongst the wet leaves.

Again Horace stopped and his large ears flickered as he strained to hear, sniffing the air, his eyes searching into the darkness.

Nothing.

He continued on but a rotten smell now filled the air.

Graveyards don't usually smell bad, do they?

The rustling came again. Horace turned abruptly.

There was another flicker of white.

Snake?

Horace gulped, his heart thumping, as he ran as fast as he could without looking back. The snake was behind him, he was sure of it, but it was slower and yet obviously successfully tracking him all the same.

Oh Charlie, what now?

Horace was shaking.

I want my ma. What would she do?

He thought hard as he tried to recall her advice.

Trust in your own abilities, Ma would say. I'm young and fast. I must keep going. Foxes never give up.

Horace ran on, hoping the snake's energy would flag and that he'd lose track.

'Aargh!' Horace stepped on something sharp. 'That really hurt.' Whatever it was had dug right in and the pain was terrible. Hobbling away from the riverside path, Horace followed the stink into a vast iron shed housing a mountain of rubbish.

I'll have to hide.

He knew a wounded fox would be at a disadvantage, but maybe the putrid smell of the rubbish would mask his scent and the snake would lose the trail.

Horace dived deep into the rubbish, where his shiny orangey-red coat blended in perfectly with the mishmash of discarded trash. Burrowing his way in, he hid himself amongst toys, clothes, furniture, packaging and broken this and that. Only his two dark amber eyes were visible as he kept watch. His paw throbbed, but he couldn't attend to it, not yet. He needed to remain completely still and keep watch.

It was difficult. Horace soon grew used to the dreadful pong of the rubbish dump and now other smells began to filter through of dead mouse and pigeon, potato, mouldy cabbage and other delicacies amongst the abandoned odds and ends and unwanted goods. Horace's tongue dripped with longing but he couldn't move. He'd have liked nothing better than to sniff out that dead mouse and gulp it down in one, but he had to stay quiet and bide his time. The snake would pass, he was sure of it, but until Zigzag McVitie showed himself, Horace couldn't move, waiting half buried in the mountain of rubbish, his right front paw throbbing painfully beneath him.

The area in front of Mount Rubbish was deserted except for a few parked vans but Horace knew there'd soon be sticks. He wouldn't be able to stay long.

A bat flew across the yard.

There was a 'hiss'.

Horace held his breath.

A black cat ran into view, its back arched and fur on end. It swerved round to look behind, its needle teeth on show and claws extended as it hissed and spat.

Horace gasped.

It's Zigzag McVitie.

It's him! He's here, right behind the cat.

Horace felt ill as he watched the long muscular body with its black zigzag stripe slide purposefully across the deserted yard in front of Mount Rubbish.

The cat hissed again in a desperate attempt to face down McVitie, while the snake effortlessly reared its head up and back into an 'S' shape, ready to strike. And then with a movement so swift it was barely visible, he shot forward and bit the cat on the neck.

There was an almighty shriek as the cat shuffled backwards, before its face slackened and it finally keeled over.

Shaking uncontrollably, Horace watched, half-buried amongst the rubbish. His breathing was shallow but he knew that if he could hear himself breathe, then so too could McVitie.

Is this where it ends?

Horace closed his eyes, wishing he could shut out the danger.

Make it go away. Make everything all right.

He let out a small whimper, his whole body shaking. Dread churned deep down in his belly, tightening his throat. He was sure the snake could hear him breathe.

I'm doomed. Goodbye, dear world!

But evidently Zigzag McVitie could not, because he continued to slide zigzag-fashion across the tarmac. His forked tongue flicked out and in, tasting the air, while Horace held his breath as he hoped and prayed that the great stench of the dump would mask the smell of wounded fox.

Holding his breath and determined not to cough or even breathe, Horace watched as the snake silently slithered through the car park towards the fence at the other end, and then out through a small snake-sized hole.

'Gone. Phew!' Horace let out a long breath and his whole body flopped with relief. Locating the dead mouse, he knocked it back in one. It had been dead for a while and contained a few maggots, which added to the flavour.

Delicious!

What else is there?

Horace sniffed out a rotting pigeon and a brown half-eaten apple, some cold spaghetti, half a meat pie and a spill of baked beans.

Lovely!

Climbing down from the rubbish mound, he sniffed at the dead cat. It didn't smell right.

What's wrong with it? That McVitie is pure poison. I really need to keep away from him.

Horace sat down on the tarmac to inspect his bleeding paw. Licking the wound clean, he flinched as splinters of glass cut his tongue, making his eyes water. Carefully he pulled out the glass and another large blob of blood formed on the swollen pad.

Feeling dizzy and faint, he looked up.

What's that?

He couldn't focus properly.

It's too dark to be a fox.

He raised his nose and sniffed as the figure moved towards him.

Do I know you?

Horace blinked repeatedly and tried squinting, determined to find out if the creature was friend or foe.

The dark shape drew closer, like a shadow ready to swamp him.

Am I in danger?

Hot and confused, Horace's brain throbbed in his skull as if it might explode. He tried to stand and put weight on the wounded paw.

Stand up and look strong – come on, you can do it!

There was a shooting pain and he staggered forward, head down and ears back, as he neared the creature side on, hoping he'd appear fit, healthy and far larger than he really was.

'Who are you? What do you want?' he whispered, and then everything went black.

Twelve

Horace hit the ground with a thud, weak with the loss of blood from his wounded paw.

'You all right, sonny?' He heard a voice.

Who's that?

Horace opened his eyes a fraction, his head pounding.

Grey gritty ground and then four dark paws with blunt claws?

He strained to get a better look. Following up from the blunt claws, he saw four dark legs and an underbelly of greying fur, topped off by a dark red coat.

It's a shabby old fox with a dark coat.

And this fox was standing over him, staring down into his face.

Horace tried to get up, baring his teeth. He gave a sharp hacking bark and a warning snarl as his paws scraped the tarmac.

The dark fox lowered his head a little and stepped back. 'Steady on, it's all right,' he said, half his teeth blunt or missing. 'You fainted, that's all.' He peered down at Horace. 'You're too pale around the eyes and that paw of yours don't look too clever.'

'Who are you?'

'The name's Johnny Red. What's your name, sonny?'

Horace stared at the dark fox's gappy mouth. 'What happened to your teeth?'

'Well, I'm no spring fox, you might say.' Johnny swished his thin bony tail. 'I've survived a fair few winters, mind. It helps, living round here.'

'I've never been anywhere like this before.'

'No one forgets their first rubbish dump.'

'Is this where you live?'

'No, not quite – it's too brightly lit for my liking, but I'm not too far away.' He nodded towards the floodlights that lit up the dump. 'I do stay close to the source though.'

'Sauce?'

'Source of food.'

'Oh yes, of course.'

'You don't know much. You got a name, sonny, or shall I have to call you Old Hopalong?'

'Horace – Horace Fox.'

Johnny took a closer look at Horace's wounded paw. 'Well, Horace, you need to rest up a while.'

'But I don't have a while. I need to find my friend and then —'

'Look, you don't rest that paw, you're gonna get yourself in trouble. You really need your four paws. Come on, get up – see if you can stand on it.'

Johnny stepped back to let Horace stand on his own four feet.

With a struggle, Horace managed to stand on three of his paws and gently tested the fourth.

'Now walk up and down.'

Horace could only hobble. He sat back down with his shoulders slumped.

'Not to worry, it just needs a day's rest and then you'll be right as rain.'

'But I don't have a day.'

'You don't rest that foot, sonny, and you won't have any more days at all. You'll be attacked before you know it, won't be able to escape, and there'll be no more Horace Fox. Rest up for a day and then you can get off as fast as you like.'

They left the bright lights of the dump and squeezed through a gap at the corner of the railings along the edge of the graveyard. At the foot of a large cedar tree, hidden by a bush, lay Johnny's foxhole.

'Hang back a moment.' Johnny squeezed through the hole and then a minute later called out, 'You can come in now.'

Horace limped through into a long tunnel. 'You sure like to dig, Johnny,' he said.

'Keep coming now, boy.'

Horace squeezed through another hole.

'Easy does it,' Johnny said.

Horace plopped through and fell onto a soft cushioned

floor covered in scraps of material. Johnny's den was a generous round chamber, the walls decorated with colourful shiny sweet wrappers.

Horace's eyes widened. 'I've never seen a den like this before.'

'I can't remember the last time I saw something new. There's a lot to be said for being young,' Johnny said with a gappy smile. 'Now then, you have a good old rest there, young Horace.'

Horace's eyelids were heavy. 'Don't let me sleep too long. I need to keep moving.'

Johnny nodded. 'Don't you worry, sonny, I'll see you do.'

Horace fell into a deep sleep for a good few hours and then woke with a wail.

'It's all right. You're all right, sonny. You're dreaming.' Johnny nudged Horace's shoulder. Horace gazed around the glittering den, as he tried to remember how he'd got there. 'Don't worry, Horace, you're safe.'

Horace's breathing steadied. 'Oh Johnny, you've got no idea. I saw the snake – Zigzag McVitie. He was about to strike.'

Johnny nodded. 'Yes, but he didn't – he didn't get you. Look, sonny, everyone has an enemy from time to time. Just remember you're a good fox and you deserve good things to happen. Remember that. You can't let this snake get the better of you. You're stronger than you think and you must stay strong. How's that paw of yours?'

Horace tested his wounded foot. 'It's better than before. I'm sure I can run. I really must get going.'

'But it's daylight. You can't go out in daylight.'

'I've no choice. I need to get on. I need to find my friend, Charlie Boom. Have you heard of him? He's a bit older than me, and he has a thick fluffy coat and tail and a chipped left tooth.'

Johnny shook his head. 'I can't think of anyone with a chipped tooth.'

'Well, can you tell me how to get back to the river?'

'You're really going out in daylight? Bear in mind you're already in fox paradise, next to the dump. It doesn't get much better than this!'

'It is rather special, but I need a place of my own and if I can get to Twickenham before sunrise on Friday, I can claim the home that should be mine.'

'Go on.'

'There's a den – a very swish den or so I've been told – in the grounds of Strawberry Hill House and it should be mine if I only claim it in time.'

'A very swish den, you say. Well, that's certainly worth claiming. Of course, I have no cubs of my own – well, none that I know of – so there's no one to whom I can pass on my own rather nice place.'

'Johnny, you're fighting fit. You don't need to worry about that.'

Johnny looked down and sighed. 'I'm an old fox and life can be lonely. You know, once the fur thins and the teeth start falling out, the vixens don't want to know. I've had a good life but my days are numbered.'

'Don't talk like that, Johnny.'

'No, really, once the teeth go, you go, simple as that.'

Horace peered into Johnny's mouth. 'You've got five good teeth.'

Johnny gave a gappy grin. 'You're a good fox, Horace – remember that.'

'I know! Why don't you come with me?'

Johnny shook his head. 'My days of adventuring are over. My legs are rickety, my joints ache, my claws are blunt and my teeth are loose. I'd be a burden to you.'

'No, you wouldn't.'

'Sonny, these days I travel only in my head, but what a journey I have!' Johnny winked. 'Imagination goes a long way when the body grows old but the mind still flies. You go, Horace. You go and claim your Strawberry House, but if it doesn't work out, come back. You'll always be welcome here. Think of it as your Plan B.'

'Plan B?'

'Plan B is what you follow if Plan A doesn't work out. Go and claim Strawberry House.' Johnny led the way out of the foxhole by the cedar tree, through the graveyard, past the flowers and balloons and the dump to a crack in the fence at the far side. Part of Horace didn't want to leave the old fox. He'd been so kind, but he knew he had to get on. He had to give it his best shot for Charlie's sake if nothing else. It was daylight now with a crisp white winter sky.

They ducked around the back of the vast shed that housed Mount Rubbish.

'The sticks are busy eating. It's a good time to scoot through and out of here.' Johnny gave a friendly nod. 'Good luck, sonny.' Horace smiled and bowed.

Thirteen

Gritting his teeth, Horace squeezed through a gap in the fence and ran as best he could on his wounded paw, which turned out to be more of a hoppity jog, but at least he was back out there covering ground, searching for Charlie, on his way to Twickenham.

Returning to the riverside, he skulked amongst the trees and bushes lining the path, doing his best to remain hidden in the daylight. Passing offices and houses, he went under another bridge and then followed along the edge of a vast walled garden. He wanted to see more, but the wall was too high.

On the opposite side of the river stood a splendid-looking mansion.

Could that be Strawberry Hill House?

The large rectangular building had a statue of a lion on its roof.

Surely someone would have mentioned a lion if that's the right place?

He decided it couldn't be the house he was looking for and ran on past another bridge, houses and pubs until he ran out of bushes to hide in and was forced to cross open land.

A goose on the path honked, 'Back off, fox-scum. You're not welcome here.'

Another one said, 'Get lost! We don't like you.'

Horace had had quite enough of violent geese, thank you. 'Okay, okay, I get the message. Just tell me the way to Twickenham?'

After returning to the safety of the water, the geese looked at one another as if they needed permission to speak.

Meanwhile a swan flicked its head, gesturing towards the other side of the river. 'It's over that bridge and keep going. You're nearly there.'

Horace ran towards the bridge, climbed the steps at the side and crossed.

On the other side he came to a road and after looking both ways, he ran for it.

Made it!

He puffed out his white chest because every road safely

crossed felt like an achievement. Sprinting down a slipway, he was back at the river where the path was once again lined with trees and bushes on either side.

Oh no!

There were sticks ahead with a dog off the lead. Horace tensed all over, with gritted teeth and his ears back, and then moved to the side, hoping to skulk past because the last thing he needed was another fight with a stupid dog. Luckily, however, one of the sticks grabbed the mutt by its collar and held it until Horace had safely passed.

Further on, there was parkland with a large white house.

Is that it? Could that be Strawberry Hill House?

Horace ran beneath the branches of a huge and ancient tree and hurtled towards the bright white house. 'I'm here, I'm here, it's me – I've made it!' he shouted as he ran around the side, looking for a way in.

Sticks were in the way, lots of them and they all had small boxes in their hands.

'It's such a treat to be filming at Marble Hill House,' said a stick in a wide pink dress, raising her eyebrows at the sight of Horace. 'Ooh, a fox – I love foxes!'

So the white house is Marble Hill House, not Strawberry Hill House. Keep going.

Horace cut across the parkland back towards the river, but just as he found his stride a dog gave chase and then another and another. Glancing back, Horace was boggle-eyed at the sight of so many grisly dogs chasing his tail.

Honestly, have they nothing better to do?

Looking over his shoulder, he saw a large German shepherd, a baggy-faced boxer and a small patch-eyed Jack Russell, all barking and baring their teeth.

What's with all this mindless aggression and violence? I'll show you, Horace thought. *You can't catch me!*

His heart racing, he did three circuits of the park, then a

figure of eight and then ran around the bright white building twice, all with the three dogs following and more joining in.

Pandemonium, as the Bishop would say. Canine chaos. They're all stupid. I am the fox – and what can foxes do better than almost anyone?

Aiming at the fence, Horace found a small gap, squashed himself flat to the ground and squeezed out to safety and calm.

Only the Jack Russell followed. Horace knew that breed.

Ma said they're natural born ratters and can despatch a rodent with one swift bite. Don't worry, because you have longer legs and you're faster, she said. Forget him.

Horace pelted across the grass and the Jack Russell gave chase, snapping at Horace's heels. Just when the dog could no longer keep up with the pace and was falling behind, a whistle sounded.

'Harry, get back here this instant!' shouted a stick, and head drooping, the Jack Russell turned tail with one last pathetic yap.

Out of breath, Horace sat and rested for a moment.

Thank goodness for that! It's nice and peaceful now that dog has gone at last.

He was in a large garden with a pond and numerous plants in pots.

Sniffing the air, he detected something fleshy and festering in one of the pots and pulled out a perfectly good goldfish.

Why would you bury such a tasty snack?

Thirsty, he headed over to the pond. Taking a deep breath, he paused and looked down at his throbbing paw. He'd overdone it, run too far, too fast, when it still had to properly heal, but what could he do? Time was running out and he still hadn't found Charlie.

Drink – it'll help.

He bent down to take a sip, but . . .

What was that?

Out of the corner of his eye at the far end, hidden in the reeds, he thought he caught a glimpse of something white and black, something that flickered.

Was that a forked tongue?

Horace stared until it was only too obvious that it *was* indeed the coiled black and white body of Zigzag McVitie, swiftly unravelling and heading in his direction.

Fourteen

Trembling all over, his eyes wide and his heart thumping, Horace staggered back as Zigzag McVitie rose up ready to strike from amongst the reeds at the edge of the pond.

Silently and with total focus, the snake whipped back and lashed out, lunging towards Horace who leapt away, escaping McVitie's evil fangs by a whisker.

Not put off one bit, McVitie rose up and pulled back in his deadly ready-to-strike 'S' shape.

Again the snake whipped forward and Horace dodged back and sideways. Once again McVitie's lunge had nowhere to go. The snake fell forwards and hit the ground – a stark black and white rope against the green grass.

'I'll get you nexxxt time, you pitiful trash-guzzzler.'

Ignoring the snake's pathetic insult, Horace darted back to the low hole in the fence through which he had come. Panting and stressed, he scraped his belly along the dirt and squeezed back through to the other side. Back in the park, he jumped through bushes, ran past the bright white house and bolted across the grass to another gateway, past a café and a playground and along a road where a car was backing out of a driveway directly into his path. With its headlights on, it was coming right at him. Panicking, Horace dived to the side and landed straight in a puddle. Drenched, he shook the water from his coat and then checked back for McVitie's telltale markings. Sticks with dogs were coming along behind him.

Avoid them, but where now?

Stay close to the river.

He needed to get his bearings or he'd never find Strawberry Hill, but the path by the river had run out, leaving only a high brick wall closing off all access.

It's too high. Is there a gap underneath?

No, he couldn't go under it so he jogged around the side where he found a gate that was heavily barred.

There's space beneath it.

Horace tested the gap under the gate with his head. He could just about make it so squeezed through.

Back on his feet, his mouth fell open at the sight of a lush city jungle full of tropical plants.

'Every day something new.'

A shrill voice said, 'What *are* you on about?'

Another voice said, 'That red one down there looks completely crackers to me.'

In a tree high above Horace sat three bright green parakeets.

'Hello there,' Horace said. 'I wonder if you can help me. There's a black and white snake on my tail – have you ladies maybe seen him?'

The parakeets grew restless on their perch. 'You're talking about Zigzag McVitie?'

'Yes, I'm afraid I am.'

'We've heard of him but we haven't seen him.'

'No, well, that's good. I don't want to see him either! How far is it to Twickenham?'

'Twickenham?!' they all screeched at once.

'Well, you're right here, babycakes,' the first parakeet said.

And the second parakeet confirmed, 'This *is* Twickenham, sunshine!'

'*Really?* Why, it's beautiful.'

The parakeets shrieked with laughter. 'It's not all like this, you know.'

'Have you heard of Strawberry Hill House?'

The parakeets nodded. 'It's absolutely lovely with plenty of fruit trees.'

'Am I nearly there then?'

The parakeets gave a sudden ear-piercing squawk and the whole lot of them took off, their green wings spread wide as they made their escape.

Alarmed, Horace spun round and saw why – *snake!*

Zigzag McVitie was right behind him, his lower body coiled and his neck pulled back. Instantly, he shot forward, ready to strike.

Dodging back, his heart pumping, Horace turned and fled. Slipping across a muddy bank and around the end of a wall into another garden he crossed the lawn and hurled himself through a hole in the fence and into another garden, this one leading down to a boat mooring. Horace jumped the fence and ran back up a slope towards the road where he saw a white pub with a picture of a swan on its sign.

Diving under a gate into a more formal garden laid out with hedging and ponds and large urns dotted along the path by the river, he shot through to the end where he stopped at the sight of a magnificent fountain. Bright white statues of sticks, all naked, hovered over a large pond with lily pads. The statues seemed to glow, like ghosts in the daytime – how strange the sticks looked without their usual coverings. Behind them was a large pile of rocks, topped off with two galloping winged horses and another naked stick. It felt like another world, a strange dreamlike place he didn't understand.

Fascinating, but I really must get on.

'Aargh!' There was a sudden sharp pain in his neck.

What was that?

No, I don't believe it. He got me!

It was a quick bite that had barely scratched him, but as Horace turned, he found Zigzag McVitie primed and ready to strike again.

'No!' Horace yelled, only too aware that he couldn't escape.

The snake whipped forward, and at the same time as if from nowhere another fox jumped out and leapt across, knocking McVitie to the ground.

Seizing his chance, Horace dived on the snake and grabbing his neck between his sharp young fangs, bit down, gripping the snake every bit as firmly as he'd once seen Charlie hold the weasel.

'Well done, Horace, I knew you had it in you. I am so proud.'

Am I hearing right? Can it be true? Is it really you?

Horace peeked over his shoulder, afraid that it might not be who he hoped it was.

'*Charlie!*' A surge of happiness flooded his entire body. 'I don't believe it.' Horace was so surprised he forgot what or rather who he had in his mouth and let the snake go.

McVitie took his chance and the foxes turned to see his black and white body slink away into a heap of fallen leaves.

'Quick!' Charlie pounced on the tip of the snake's tail but his grip wasn't firm enough and he fell back as McVitie yanked himself free. '*Get him!*' Charlie shouted, and Horace bared his teeth, tracking the flurry of leaves as McVitie slithered beneath them.

Horace pounced and – *gotcha!* – locked onto the snake's tail but McVitie whipped around, twisting his head back ready to strike.

This time Horace saw it coming. Jumping back, he swung McVitie round with all his strength and then let go, flinging the snake's body out like a fishing line.

'Aargh!' McVitie screamed as his head hurtled towards the trunk of a large tree.

Horace held his breath.

Thwack!

'Oh dear.' Horace bit his lip. 'I didn't mean for that to happen. What have I done?'

In front of him, a quivering McVitie was left hanging by his two nasty fangs, which were now firmly stuck in the dark gnarly bark of the tree.

'Help, get me down,' the snake begged with some difficulty.

'Well, I don't see how we can,' Charlie said, 'not without you being defanged.'

McVitie gave a strangled sob. 'How could you? My preciousss teeth, now blunt like a ussselesss tool.'

'Sorry about that,' Horace said, 'but then again, I'm not really sorry because now you can't kill me.'

'Whatever . . .' the snake hissed. 'Jussst get me down.'

'You're happy to be defanged?' Charlie said.

'Do what you have to do.' McVitie's throat made a gurgling sound.

'He won't make much of an assassin any more, thank goodness,' Horace said, 'but how will he eat without his teeth?'

'Have you not seen a snake eat? It's disgusting,' Charlie said. 'They swallow stuff whole. I've seen a fluffy baby rabbit disappear in one bite, its little feet still moving under the stretched snakeskin.'

'Eww, and he has the cheek to comment on us eating from bins!'

'Aww, gimme a break,' McVitie said. 'You foxxxes aren't ssso great.'

'Yeah, well at least we don't poison anyone.'

'I'm bored of all thisss chit-chat and my neck hurtsss,' McVitie said. 'Leave me dangling and I'll die anyhow. Get me down whatever way you can.'

'I'll try, if you like.' Stepping forward, Charlie yanked the snake by the tail.

There was a clean crisp *snap!* and McVitie fell to the ground in a miserable black and white heap – his two precious pearly white fangs still firmly stuck in the gnarly bark of the tree . . .

Horace took a deep breath. He couldn't help feeling just the tiniest bit sorry for McVitie now he'd lost his teeth.

Life isn't long when you don't have your teeth.

Fifteen

Together at last, Horace and Charlie watched amazed as the magnificent fountain with its naked stick statues and galloping winged horses erupted into life as plumes of water sprayed up and out in a glorious display.

'Look at that! It's like the fountain's celebrating our victory over the snake,' Charlie said.

'I can't believe it – I thought I'd never see you again,' Horace said. 'What happened? Where did you go?'

Charlie shook his head. 'Long story, mate.'

McVitie groaned. 'What ith a thnake without hith fangth?'

'What did he say?' Horace asked.

Charlie grinned. 'Without his front teeth, he seems to have developed a lisp.'

'They'll grow back then I'll finith the job. It'th not over yet.' McVitie rolled onto his front and once more slid away into a pile of fallen leaves.

'What the heck? Get him!' Charlie shouted.

Horace leapt on the snake's tail and held firm.

'We're not done with you yet,' Charlie said.

'We're not?' Horace said.

Charlie, baring his one and a half fangs, eyeballed the snake. 'You know the whereabouts of this Strawberry House, McVitie?'

The snake kept quiet as his cold yellow eyes tried to out-stare Charlie.

'You will show us,' Charlie said. 'Show us the way or you'll lose more than your two front teeth. You'd make a nice handbag or pair of shoes for a stick.'

'I'll thow you the way,' the snake hissed, 'though it'll be little help when you thtill have to deal with Badger Burnhard – no one beatth Badger Burnhard.'

'You just let us worry about that,' Charlie said.

Zigzag McVitie's tongue flicked in and out beneath his bleeding gums.

'You lead,' Charlie said, 'but don't forget we're right behind you, so no funny business. And remember, you ain't got the fangs to help you no more.'

McVitie slipped ahead past the fountains and statues and left through the gate with Horace and Charlie close behind.

As they followed, Charlie took a good long look at Horace. 'You look quite the fox these days,' he said. 'You've grown up, you have.'

'I thought I'd lost you forever. Where did you go? What happened?'

'What a nightmare – you have no idea . . . One minute I'm swimming for it in the river with that brainless dog barking at me from the bank, and the next thing I know I get out, start running, the dog grabs me, gets a bite out of my behind and I manage to shake off the stupid mutt and escape, but he keeps following. So I do a quick left and dive through a hedge into a garden. The place is nice, feels safe, know what I mean? I reckon I can hang around here, wait for the dog to pass. I can hear him barking like a loon on the other side of the hedge, but he doesn't find me.

'Anyway, I'm bleeding, not in a good place health-wise, know what I mean, so I need to rest up, lick my wounds. I've got my ears pricked in case I hear you come by. And I'm happy like that, minding my own business, taking time out to get better, because really if you ain't got your health, then what have you got? A wounded fox can quickly become a dead fox if he don't take care of himself. So I find a quiet corner, nice and sheltered, shielded from view and the elements, tuck myself in down a crack between a fence and a shed, and I'm quite happy there. I clean out the wound and can't help but take a quick nap.'

'That all sounds quite positive so far – what went wrong?'

'Well, I had a very nice sleep. I remember dreaming of a beautiful vixen I used to know and a den in the country – lovely it was – but then I wake up and find a plastic loop being tightened around my neck.'

'No!'

'Yup. Terrifying, and I didn't know what it was. Anyway, turns out to be Animal Rescue, would you believe! "I don't want to be rescued. I don't need rescuing," I keep telling them, but they never understand anything, these sticks, and they certainly don't listen.'

'So what did the stick do with you?'

'There was this other old stick with white hair and a tartan dressing gown.'

'Tartan dressing gown? I know the one. She leaves food out in a bowl.'

'Yes, she does.'

'I thought she was all right, that stick.'

'Yeah, you're not wrong, just a little bit interfering in my humble opinion.'

'What happened next?'

'Well, the old stick must have come out to the garden, seen me wounded and contacted Animal Rescue. Another stick then turns up with the plastic loop on a long pole, puts the loop over my head and around my neck, tightens it and then drags me from my lovely cosy resting place and shoves me in a small cage, which the sticks called a "pet carrier".'

'We are not pets!'

'No, exactly. And then I get carried in the cage by the stick from Animal Rescue to a white van.'

'Not a *white van*?'

'Yes, a white van! So I'm shoved in the back and the stick from Animal Rescue gets in the front and drives me away – a long, long way away.'

'And then what?'

'I'm taken out into a white room with bright lights on the ceiling and a stick dressed in green looks at every part of me.'

'Every part?'

'Every part.'

'That's not right.'

'Then they put me out. I thought I'd died, but I came back round and my wound felt funny, sort of tight. They'd done something, fixed it somehow. I have to admit it did the trick and to be fair I had lovely food in there and plenty of it. They took care of me. Only trouble was, I was fretting because I knew you were out here on your own and you needed my help.'

'But now you're back. How did you find your way?'

'They kept me a while, then they looked at me again, stuck me back in the "pet-carrier", back in the van and back to the old stick's garden.'

'What did she do?'

'She was smiling and clapping her hands.'

'Told you – she's all right that one.'

'She even put out a bowl of food.'

'Meat in jelly, was it? That is one kind stick.'

'But I needed to get on. I needed to find you, make sure

you were okay and help you sort out that blooming nasty snake.'

Zigzag McVitie hissed and his tongue flickered. 'My teeth will grow back and then you'll be thorry. You'll all be thorry.'

'By the way, where are we now, snake?' Charlie said.

'Eel Pie Island to the left.' Zigzag McVitie nodded towards an oval-shaped island with a small footbridge linking it to the mainland. It was certainly pie-shaped and covered in trees, houses and boatbuilders' sheds.

'Eel pie – that sounds good,' Horace said.

'Oh yes, I love a few wriggly eels,' Charlie said.

Walking away from the river, they took a small lane by a church to a cobbled street where they found a small shop with a sign of a big steaming pie.

'Let's check round the back for black sacks and spillages,' Charlie said.

Trooping round the back, they found a spotless yard with nothing to be had.

'Could we not burst in the front door just as a stick is leaving?' Horace said.

'Are you mad?' Charlie said. 'Us foxes survive by skulking in the shadows, you know that.'

Horace, hungry as ever, sighed. How he longed for a fresh hot pie as good as the sticks ate, but he knew it was hopeless. Charlie was right, they should always stay as hidden as possible.

Further along the cobbled street they came to an old white building with a painted sign showing a red fox.

Horace stared up at the sign. 'Well, would you look at that! It must be a good omen.'

Again they checked round the back for discarded food, but the bins had recently been emptied and there was a complete lack of any delicious smells, rotten or otherwise.

McVitie, however, who had the sense to look elsewhere,

located something alive and edible in the damp by the far wall. He swallowed it whole, and the foxes watched in disgust as a frog-shaped lump, still kicking, travelled slowly down the snake's ropy neck.

'You really should learn to chew your food,' Horace said.

The snake flicked his tongue out and looked away with disdain.

'Which way now, McVitie?' Charlie said.

The snake looked vague as if digesting his dinner was fogging his brain.

'Stop messing, McVitie, you know the way.' Horace was pacing up and down.

Charlie caught McVitie by the neck. 'Get on with it before I wrap you around a lamp post and tie you in a knot.'

'Very well, if I mutht, though you could give one a moment to digetht one'th food.' McVitie slid ahead down a narrow street and back towards the river. Taking a private road in front of some garages he went over a wall into the grounds of a block of flats. They were still heading in the right direction along the river, which Horace found comforting.

The snake slid on, over another wall into another garden, across a lawn, and through a gap in the fence, and so they continued – the snake and the two foxes passing through the grounds of at least twenty homes, and a school and another house and a public park where they met sticks fishing on the riverbank.

'Wah, a snake!' One of the sticks jumped to his feet.

Ignoring the sticks, McVitie, Horace and Charlie travelled on past a war memorial, a bowling green, a children's playground and a café, until they came to a gate where McVitie paused.

'It's juth up there,' he said.

'Keep going then,' Charlie said. 'What's keeping you?'

The snake backed away, his yellow eyes wide and fearful.

'What are you doing?' Horace said.

McVitie backed up further towards the fence. 'Have merthy on me, pleath. It'th Badger Burnhard. I failed him. He will kill me.'

'Yeah, and we'll kill you if you fail us,' Charlie said. 'Move it!'

But McVitie shrank even further back from the road onto a grass verge.

'My dad left this den to me,' Horace said. 'Badger Burnhard has no right to my property. It's time for you to do the right thing.'

Charlie snarled, spit dripping from his chipped fang.

McVitie sighed. 'Very well, if I really mutht.'

They had come to a roundabout with yet another road to cross. Listening and looking, they waited for a break in the rumble of the traffic. 'Go for it!' Horace shouted and they made a run for it. *Not* the recommended way to cross a road, of course, but for foxes, crossing roads always involves an element of luck and foolish daring.

Horace and Charlie made it across, but McVitie was hit. The end of his tail was squished by the wheel of a car and stuck to the tarmac of the road.

'Leave him,' Charlie said. 'We haven't time to mess around.'

Horace shook his head. 'I can't just leave him there, and besides we need him. He's our guide.' Using his snout, Horace gently peeled McVitie's flattened tail from the road surface. 'Can you move?'

McVitie tried to slide forward, but jolted and dropped. He rose up again, jolted and dropped.

'He's too slow,' Charlie said.

'We have to help him.' Carefully, Horace took the wounded snake in his mouth and draped him like a scarf round Charlie's neck. 'There, quite suits you,' he said.

McVitie dipped his head. 'I've never felt tho athamed.'

'What did he say?' Charlie said.

'No idea,' Horace said. 'Don't worry about it.'

They found themselves at a crossroads with houses to the left and right, and a long straight road ahead.

'It'th up there on the left.' McVitie nodded towards a building shielded by trees.

Horace smiled. 'We're nearly there – we've made it! Will it be anything like I imagined?' He ran ahead, keen to see his den, his very swish den, somewhere near Strawberry Hill House which he'd been told looked like a castle.

There were large trees set behind a long grey fence, and further on some fancy iron railings, and then it finally came into view – a beautiful creamy white castle with turrets and arched windows and a grand cloistered entrance.

Wide-eyed, Horace stopped short and his mouth fell open. 'Wow, would you look at that! It's completely and utterly wonderful.'

Charlie whistled. 'Now *that* is what I call a castle.'

Horace jogged ahead through the tall iron gates straight up to the solid wooden door and stared up at the brass knocker high above his head.

'What are you doing?' Charlie said. 'Foxes are backdoor sorts. We never knock on any door or deliberately show ourselves. It's not in our nature.'

'I just wanted to see the main entrance, that's all.' Horace turned, ready to head round the back, but something was wrong.

I don't feel right.

'Charlie, I—'

Horace collapsed and his head hit the door with a loud *thwack!*

'*Horace?*' Charlie gasped and was about to run to his friend, but the door opened. Someone must have heard Horace hit the door as he fell.

Quickly, Charlie (still with McVitie around his neck) backed into the shadows at the side.

A stick stood in the doorway, tall and pale with a sharp nose and even sharper cheekbones. He frowned as he shoved Horace with his boot.

Horace didn't flinch – in fact he did not move at all.

'Good heavens, how peculiar. There's a dead fox on the doorstep!' the stick said. 'How on earth did that get there? Can someone remove it? Where's the head gardener? Summon the gardener and tell him to bring a shovel.'

The stick gave Horace another sharp kick.

Charlie gulped. *'Please get up, Horace!'*

But still Horace did not move and the stick looked down with a scowl on his face, before turning away and closing the door.

Sixteen

Horace lay motionless on the doorstep of Strawberry Hill House.

As soon as the stick had closed the front door, Charlie scurried forward and used his head and the full force of his body to shove Horace into the nearest bush.

'*Horace*, wake up!' Charlie licked and pawed Horace's face. 'He's not responding. What's the matter with him?' Charlie listened at Horace's chest. 'His heart's beating and he's breathing. Why won't he wake up?'

McVitie slid off Charlie's neck and landed with a jagged awkward bump. His tongue flickered as he smelt Horace's neck. 'I think I know the cauth,' he said, lisping as usual, thanks to his lack of teeth.

'Yes, and what is it?' Charlie said.

'I could tell you, only you're going to have to promith you won't get mad.' There was fear in the snake's yellow eyes as he edged away from Charlie.

'All right, just tell me – what is it?'

'I bit him.'

'You *what!*' Immediately, Charlie was at McVitie's throat. 'You did what?'

'You promithed you wouldn't get mad.'

'That was before I heard what you'd done.'

'It was only a thmall shallow bite. It happened before you arrived in the garden with the fountainth and before my fangth got knocked out. There mutht be some poithon in him. Only a little, I'd thay – not enough to kill him.'

Charlie took a deep breath. 'Will he survive?'

'Yeth, I'm sure he will if he'th lucky and he theemth lucky.'

'What can we do? Please tell me there's something we can do?'

'It doethn't look too theriouth. He's not thwollen and he's not vomiting.'

'*He's completely knocked out!*'

'It could be worth – a lot worth. I think he'll be fine.'

Horace's head moved slightly, his eyes flickered and he retched.

'He's been sick,' Charlie said, '*and look at his neck* – it's swelling up. It's huge! He looks like a snake that's swallowed a rabbit. What can we do?'

'He needth an antidote to counteract the poithon.'

'You mean to stop poison working? Where do we get this antidote?'

'I wouldn't know. Normally I jutht thrike and go.'

'You mean you normally strike and go?' Charlie paced up and down as he tried to think. He knew nothing about antidotes or where to find them but he was a fox of action and there was no way he could stand by and do nothing.

McVitie swallowed hard. His eyes bulged as he stared ahead into the distance.

'What is it?' Charlie followed the snake's eyeline to a gap in the bushes where Charlie could see a pair of light amber eyes spying on them. 'Who goes there?' Charlie said. 'Show yourself.'

There was a gentle rustle of leaves and a splash of golden light broke through the branches and Charlie's mouth fell open as the most beautiful young vixen with a lush smooth flame-red coat came into view.

'Who are you and why are you watching us?'

'I heard a commotion and I can see your friend is in a bad way.' She approached, her eyes soft and caring.

'He's been poisoned by this wretched snake.'

'I know someone who can help if you're able to move him?'

Charlie nodded. 'Yes, of course. I'll move him anywhere he needs to go.'

The vixen gestured with her soft amber eyes, indicating that they should follow.

Charlie dragged Horace along by the skin at the back of his neck, like a vixen with her cub. It was slow, strenuous work.

'Can we lay him over your back?' the vixen said.

'Let's try.'

The vixen used all her strength to push and shove Horace

onto Charlie's shoulders.

'McVitie, wrap yourself round Horace and me,' Charlie said. 'Act like you're a belt and hold him on. It's the least you can do.'

The kind young vixen led Charlie, with Horace strapped to his back by McVitie, around the edge of the castle and through trees and bushes into a corner of the grounds where the plants had grown into a wild tangle of bushes, briars and twisty branches.

'This is the place.' Shielded from general view lay a perfect foxhole next to a thick hedge.

With the vixen pulling from the front and Charlie shoving from behind, they tugged Horace through the secret entrance into an overgrown orchard full of ancient apple trees.

'Great neighbourhood,' Charlie said.

'My ma found this place. She always knows where's best.' The flame-red vixen then slipped into a dugout under a huge battered shed where an older vixen lay deep in a bed of russet leaves.

'Loveness, is that you?' The old vixen looked weary, as if they'd woken her from sleep.

Charlie set Horace down before the old vixen. 'Hello, ma'am,' he said. 'This is my dear friend Horace, and as you can see he's in a bad way. We really need your help. Please tell me there's something you can do?'

The old vixen eyed McVitie. 'You!' she said, narrowing her cloudy eyes. 'You again – you've got a nerve, coming back here.'

'Oh Ma, not now,' the beautiful young vixen said.

'Shush, child,' said the old vixen. She stared back at McVitie. 'You did this, no doubt? It certainly looks like your handiwork.'

McVitie squirmed. 'It wath only a thmall bite.'

'Well, at least I know what I'm dealing with.' She leaned

over Horace and inspected his eyes. 'There's some swelling.' She sniffed at his neck. 'Well, I've dealt with this before, so I know what to do. Don't worry, I have something.' She searched through the leaves, sniffing out something she had stashed away, and after a while dug out a small brown dried lump of something so stinky it had to be good.

'Let me do it,' the beautiful young vixen said.

The old vixen gave a small nod. 'Very well. It's best you learn.'

With everyone gathered round to watch, the young vixen took the smelly chunk in her mouth and chewed it to soften it up. She then knelt down at Horace's side and fed the mush into his mouth, like a bird feeding its chick.

Horace gave a loud hacking cough and the goo dribbled back out.

Not put off in the least, the beautiful young vixen tried again.

A tense few minutes went by, but still Horace showed few signs of life.

Charlie crossed his legs for luck. 'Come on, Horace, you can do it – wake up!'

Finally Horace's eyelids flickered.

'Did you see that?' Charlie shouted. 'He's coming round!'

Horace moaned and scratched at his swollen neck as he opened his eyes.

Seeing the beautiful young vixen, he felt himself redden but was too weak to sit up.

My gosh, such loveliness – I've never seen such beauty!

His heart thumped as he took in her silky flame-red coat and her soft light amber eyes, the colour of sweet honeycomb. Again he tried to rise and this time managed to stagger back onto all fours before resting back down.

Charlie helped him up and finally Horace managed to puff out his fluffy white chest. 'I'm Horace – Horace Fox,' he said, gazing in wonder at the young vixen.

'How are you feeling, Horace?' the old vixen said.

'I've had better days, but then again I've had worse.' All Horace wanted to know was the name of the beauty sitting by his side and he felt himself blush inside as he struggled to think what to say. 'All of a sudden, I feel fine, I really do. I'm fit – extremely fit,' he said, hoping the beautiful young vixen would agree. 'Where am I exactly?'

'It's Strawberry Hill,' Charlie said. 'Don't you remember how we made it here to Strawberry Hill House in good time and you, being brave or more likely foolish, went straight to the front door?'

The young vixen looked at the old vixen, while the old vixen looked from Charlie to Horace. 'What did you say your name was?' the old vixen asked.

'Horace – I'm Horace Fox.' He pushed out his jaw, showing off his fine white throat. 'I've come to claim the den my father left me.'

'Well, I never.' The old vixen stared at Horace. 'You're just like your father – I should have guessed.'

'Sorry, what did you say?'

'You look like him.'

'Look like who?'

'Dickie, of course.' The old vixen smiled, revealing gappy well-worn teeth. 'I'm Claretina Foxduka. I was your father's housekeeper before he died.'

'You knew my father?'

She nodded. 'I looked after his den until Badger Burnhard kicked us out.'

'He kicked you out?'

'Yes, before Dickie had even turned cold.' Claretina looked towards the beautiful young vixen. 'This is my daughter, Loveness.'

'Loveness.' Horace felt compelled to utter the sweet sound of her name from his own lips. 'Loveness Foxduka.'

Loveness smiled.

'And I'm Charlie Boom.' Horace's best friend gave a brief bow.

Horace edged forward to do the same. He bowed towards Claretina. 'You saved my life, thank you. I am forever in your debt.' And to Loveness, Horace bowed a little more deeply. 'Thank you.'

Charlie laughed. 'You can get up now.'

'*Am* I in the right place?' Horace said. 'What exactly did my dad leave to me?'

'We'll take you there now,' Claretina said.

The line of foxes walked through the orchard to the foxhole and on into the grounds of Strawberry Hill House, where they trotted along the edge towards a large oak tree.

'This is it,' Loveness said, pointing to a foxhole at the base of the tree.

'Oh.' Horace looked from the tree towards the big house and then back again.

It was a fine tree with a broad trunk so Horace knew it had lived a good many years and was as sturdy and strong as you'd want a tree to be, but at the same time it was hardly Strawberry Hill House, which looked more like a castle.

'You look disappointed.'

'No, well, yes – is this it? Is this all my dad left me?'

'All?' Claretina shook her head as if she didn't understand how Horace could be so underwhelmed.

'What about the big creamy-coloured castle of Strawberry Hill – wasn't I left something a little more like that?'

The vixens looked at each other and laughed. 'Sticks live in that place,' Loveness said. 'They always have and they always will. But this is lovely once you get inside.'

'It's more than lovely,' Claretina said. 'It's a real home – the sort of place a fox can settle and be safe for generations to come.'

'Well, I'd better take a look then,' Horace said.

Loveness stepped away, her ears back and her tail low. 'You can't,' she said.

'Why ever not? You said it's lovely and perfect for foxes.'

'Someone's in there,' Claretina said. 'It's not safe for you right now.'

'What do you mean?'

'I'm sorry to say that Badger Burnhard has taken it.'

'But we made it here in time – long before sunrise and well before the magic hour.'

'Badger Burnhard doesn't play by the rules,' Claretina said. 'He said there was no way you'd make it here in time. He said he'd made sure of that.'

'So he thought he might as well make use of it? Are you saying someone else is living in Horace's house? We'll see about that!' Charlie aimed straight for the foxhole and dived in.

'No!' Loveness shouted and Claretina looked away, afraid of what would happen next.

There was silence for a moment, followed by the sound of muffled talking which soon turned into barking. And growling. Snarling. Grizzling.

There was crashing and banging and the sounds of desperate fighting.

Finally Charlie came back out, his coat all messed up and with claw marks across his left cheek. Moving far away from the foxhole, he sat down heavily.

'Are you all right, Charlie?' Horace went over to his friend.

'You've met Selwyn,' Claretina said, shaking her head. 'I have something for your cuts.'

'Who's Selwyn?' Horace asked.

'He's the son of Badger Burnhard and I have nothing good to say about him.'

'Well, I told him that we're here to lay claim to what is rightfully yours and he went ballistic – clawed my face and then he said, "Ask my dad".'

'He sounds like a right maniac,' Horace said. 'What do we do now?'

There was the tiniest crease in her brow as Loveness frowned. 'Natural Law is on your side,' she said, 'but you need to let Badger Burnhard know you've arrived and that you made it here in good time, long before the supposed deadline. You need to go to The Dark Hedges.'

'The Dark Hedges?' Horace's stomach tightened with worry. 'That does not sound like somewhere I'd like to go.'

Claretina stared into the distance beyond the castle-like shape of Strawberry Hill House. 'It is not a place where good things happen, but that's not to say you shouldn't go and claim what is rightfully yours. There is only one fox who can face Badger Burnhard and as the legal owner of this den that someone is you, Horace.'

Seventeen

After days spent in search of the sweet-sounding Strawberry
Hill House, Horace now had to find the scarily named Dark
Hedges.

Claretina looked at the greying sky. 'I suggest you go
sooner rather than later.'

Loveness nodded. 'I know the quickest route.'

'My dear, who said anything about you going? Badger
Burnhard is dangerous.'

'Oh Ma, they'll be far quicker with me as their guide.'

'It's not safe, my child. That Burnhard is no good and he
surrounds himself with others who are equally bad.'
Claretina gave McVitie a dirty look.

'Ma, you know I can look after myself.'

Claretina sighed. 'Show them the way then, but come back
to me, won't you?' She looked at Horace and Charlie. 'Look
after her. Don't let her come to any harm. I'm counting on
you.'

And so it was decided for Loveness to lead the way,
followed by Horace and Charlie with the wounded Zigzag
McVitie.

'I'll take McVitie this time.' Horace wanted to give Charlie a break.

'I don't mind. Really, it's no bother,' Charlie said.

'We'll take it in turns. It's only fair,' Horace said.

McVitie looked from one fox to the other. 'Well, that'th the firtht time anyone'th fought over *me*,' he lisped.

Horace lay down and McVitie slid up onto his shoulders, wrapping himself securely around Horace's neck.

'Ready?' Loveness said.

Horace, Charlie and McVitie all nodded, and Loveness took off, swift and direct, out of the gates of Strawberry Hill House. Turning left, she headed down the long and winding road towards Badger Burnhard's place, the Dark Hedges.

Leading from the front, Loveness dashed across a road and swerved round a roundabout, followed closely behind by Charlie, Horace and McVitie.

On reaching a busy built-up area they were spotted by a stick, who spilt his family-sized bag of nachos across the pavement in surprise.

Salty snacks! Horace drooled at the thought and was tempted to grab what he could, but Loveness did not pause for nachos, she did not pause for anything, and there was no way Horace would risk losing sight of her.

'Cherry trees, do you see them?' Loveness pointed her nose towards a scattering of trees. 'They mark the boundary of Badger Burnhard's territory.'

Being winter it wasn't immediately obvious but there were cherry trees in all the gardens. Badgers love cherries and eat them whole, stones and all, which then pass through their guts and out the other end along the edges of the badgers' territory. The stones then grow into cherry trees, and so it was that in springtime cheerful pink blossom would burst out all around the outer limits of Burnhard's grim and dismal kingdom, the Dark Hedges.

Loveness directed everyone down another long road, past more houses and across two zebra crossings. Finally, she turned right through tall wrought-iron gates into a grand park that opened into an avenue of huge chestnut trees, bare as skeletons in the winter gloom, marching on towards a large round pond with a golden statue in the centre.

Moving away from the road, Loveness turned right, heading for the wilder grassland. Dodging between large tufts of grass, the foxes and snake ran through tall bracken and bushes until—

'Whoa!' Loveness pulled up sharp at the sight of antlers – a herd of deer almost hidden by the bushes where they lay. An almighty stag rose to his feet and bellowed, dipping his antlers as if ready to make a run at Loveness.

Horace rushed forward to push Loveness out of the path of the stag, before himself being pulled away by Charlie. The stag gave chase, strong and powerful, and quicker than it looked, but still the foxes were faster.

Bolting across the uneven land, they escaped, keeping a sharp lookout for more deer as they continued on their way. Slowing to a steadier, more careful pace, they paddled through a flooded ditch and then trekked through a shadowy copse and across more grassland until they reached a large fenced-off area.

'If I remember rightly, this is the route.' Loveness ran around the edge, seeking a way in. There was a low hole where the grass was worn away.

'This must be it,' she said. 'I remember the shape of these trees.'

'Stop!' a voice called from behind the fence. 'I mean, halt! Who goes there?'

The voice sounded familiar. The three foxes plus snake strained to peer between the gaps in the fence to see who was talking.

Horace could make out the jerky, nervous movements of a small brown figure. 'Weasel Le Hoop, is that you?'

'Oh blast – damn and blast it!' There was the sound of a tussle as if the creature was caught in a fight, but when he finally showed himself with twigs and ivy in his fur, it seemed he'd merely got caught up in the bushes. It *was* Weasel Le Hoop. He slipped through the small hole under the fence before popping out in front of the three foxes and snake, and then stepped back in shock.

'McVitie, what are you doing?' Weasel Le Hoop was confused to find the snake draped around Horace's neck. 'Are you friends with them now? What is this – have you gone to the other side? Goodness me!'

McVitie pursed his lips and narrowed his yellow eyes, seeming unsure of what to say and rather embarrassed.

'McVitie making friends? Well, I never thought I'd see the day!' Weasel Le Hoop fidgeted as he talked as if jogging on the spot.

'Le Hoop, don't you ever stand still?' Charlie said.

'Makes me dizzy just watching him,' Loveness said.

'I don't think he can help it,' Horace said. 'Anyway, enough of watching Le Hoop – we need to keep going. Time is getting on and I must get to The Dark Hedges.'

'Oh no, you can't do that!' Le Hoop said. 'Badger Burnhard doesn't see anyone. He doesn't see anyone at all. He *hates* visitors. He hates absolutely everyone, but especially foxes. I think it's your speed really. Fast things irritate him and he doesn't like the way you filch so much food because that's less food for him – he finds that particularly irritating. Come to think of it, just about *everything* irritates him.'

'Well, that's as maybe,' Horace said, 'but I need to see him as soon as possible and I won't take no for an answer.'

'My gosh, you've changed your tune!' Le Hoop said, and Charlie grinned as Horace pressed forward and went for the hole.

'I'm going to see this Badger Burnhard before sunrise whether he likes it or not,' Horace said.

'Oh no, don't do that!' Weasel Le Hoop jumped in Horace's way, trying to stop him.

'Look, Le Hoop, we've been to Strawberry Hill. We arrived in good time, but Badger Burnhard's son, Selwyn, has moved in and refuses to leave,' Horace said. 'It's just not on, and you know that. I need to see Badger Burnhard, so kindly get out of my way!'

Weasel Le Hoop gulped. 'Right, yes, fair enough, you do have a point there.'

'Of course, we have a point.' Charlie shoved Le Hoop aside.

Horace went straight through the hole with McVitie around his neck, closely followed by Loveness and Charlie and finally Le Hoop.

On the other side, they found themselves in dense wild woodland that at first looked like a solid wall of trees, but as the group drew nearer, they realised there was a way in past a large hollow trunk that looked as if it had been struck by lightning.

Loveness shivered. 'There's something spooky about this place.'

'Stay right behind me,' Horace said, 'and you'll be fine.'

Charlie ran ahead of both of them, keen to lead from the front, while Weasel Le Hoop dragged along at the back with his shoulders hunched.

'I must warn you, you're making a huge mistake. Don't go any further,' he said. 'You really must turn back. Oh dearie me, this is not good – not good at all.'

Ignoring him, the three foxes plus snake plus weasel trailing behind moved on, deeper and deeper into the wild wood in search of the Dark Hedges.

The forest floor lay thick with rotting leaves while the trees above were dark spiky structures against the inky night sky. The three foxes plus snake plus weasel balanced along a log and crossed an icy river before venturing on to a small clearing between thorny bushes which led to an avenue of towering black trees.

'I think this is it,' Loveness said. 'Am I right?' she asked Weasel Le Hoop.

'You might be.' He looked away as if afraid to confirm that or indeed anything at all.

'Stop messing, Le Hoop – is this the place or not?' Charlie snarled, showing his chipped left fang.

Weasel Le Hoop sighed. 'Very well then. Yes, it's here, through the trees and then a bit further on and down.' He nodded in a vague direction.

Loveness crept forward, followed by Horace plus snake, Charlie and Weasel Le Hoop, all treading carefully. There was silence, except for the odd crack of a twig underfoot.

'Doesn't look much like hedges,' Horace whispered.

The bare trees with their tangle of muscular branches made a fearsome and confusing fortress wall. A shiver ran down Horace's spine and he imagined the branches closing in on him and never letting go. He swallowed hard. He needed to hold his nerve.

I can get through this! As Ma always says, a fox must never give up, whatever the danger.

They battled through and at the end of the trees, the ground dipped down into a large ditch leading to a wall of holly bushes.

'Now what?' Horace looked around for a way through. Suddenly a fierce gust of wind blew the leaves round in the ditch like a dusty whirlpool, something that could whip you up, drag you down and never let you go.

Buffeted by the strong wind, Loveness rocked on her feet.

And then suddenly the foxes' ears all pricked. They knew they were not alone.

Silence, except for another biting blast of wind, and then two huge lumbering badgers appeared from amongst the holly bushes. Glowering at the visitors, they filled the space with their hefty shoulders, black eyes and snouts, while their thick black and white striped faces reminded Horace of witches' toothpaste (if witches bother with toothpaste at all, that is).

Weasel Le Hoop took a sharp intake of breath. 'See, I told you, you're not welcome – no one is,' he said. 'There's still time. You can turn back now and everything will be fine.'

Charlie nudged Le Hoop forward. 'You know the badgers – talk to them. Get us in there.'

'I really don't want to do that. It's not a good idea.'

The badgers loomed over them, making their hefty presence known.

'Get on with it, Le Hoop.' Charlie once again pushed the

weasel forward.

'I say, hello, how is everyone?' Weasel Le Hoop was his usual jittery, fidgeting ball of nervous energy.

The largest badger had one shiny black eye, while the other eye socket was hollow. He turned his good and only eye towards Le Hoop. 'Not you again.' He made a face and shook his head. 'I don't know who your foxy friends are, but they're not welcome here – no one is, no one ever has been, and you should know that by now. I suggest you go right now and take your pathetic pals with you before we turn a little bit nasty, know what I mean?'

'Yeah, and we can be proper nasty.' The other badger's snout dripped with snot as he scratched his hairy backside with his long claws.

'We're here to see Badger Burnhard,' Horace said. 'It's most important that we see him and we can't leave until we do. There, I've said it.' He looked at Charlie for backup.

'He doesn't do visitors,' One Eye said. 'You know that.'

'Tell him it's Horace Fox,' Weasel Le Hoop said.

'Yeah, and so what?' One Eye scoffed. 'You think he cares who you lot are?'

'I *demand* to see Badger Burnhard,' Horace said.

The badgers laughed.

'Like that will work,' Dripping Snout said. 'Do not disturb Badger Burnhard – that's all the advice you need to lead a long and happy life.'

Horace stood extra tall, his shoulders back and his bright white chest puffed out and handsome. 'I demand to see Badger Burnhard. I've been to Strawberry Hill. I arrived on time – well, early actually, many hours before sunrise – and now I'm here with a message from his son.'

The badgers gave each other a look and then stared hard at Horace.

'You've spoken to Selwyn?' One Eye said.

'Yes,' Charlie interrupted. 'We've had a long conversation and Selwyn very much wants us to meet his father.'

The badgers looked at each other again and shrugged.

Dripping Snout scratched his armpit and sniffed. 'Hold on a minute,' he said, 'that snake – ain't that Zigzag McVitie? What you doing with McVitie round your neck?'

McVitie's tongue flickered. 'Ignore everything they've thaid.'

'What's the matter with your teeth?' One Eye said. 'You're talking funny.'

'His teeth have all gone,' Dripping Snout said. 'He can't speak proper. That's tragic, that is – everyone needs teeth.'

McVitie hissed. 'You mutht tell Badger Burnhard that Thigthag McVitie has arrived. Tell him I've brought "*The One*".'

'Thigthag?' The badgers clutched their bellies and laughed.

'Stop it!' Horace said. 'You're being unkind. No one laughs at you two just because you've only got the one eye and you've got a drippy nose all the time. You should be ashamed of yourselves.'

He looked over his shoulder at the snake, still wrapped around his neck. 'See, I'm backing you up, McVitie, so you'd better not double-cross me.'

'You jutht watch thith thpace,' McVitie lisped. 'It will be my methage that getth uth in to meet Badger Burnhard, you'll thee.'

A sudden tremor shook the ground.

'What was that?' Horace said.

'It's the boss.' There was fear in One Eye's one eye.

High above them in the branches of a tree, a tawny owl spun its head as it looked from the foxes to the badgers to the gap in the hedge. Obviously alarmed, it spread its wings and took flight.

Dripping Snout shook his head and shuffled away through

the holly bushes and out of sight. The night sky grew even darker with a mere sliver of moon and the air was icy as the foxes waited. And then before they could see him, they smelt him and felt yet another rumbling tremor. Fear showed on everyone's face.

'Foolish, foolish foxes.' One Eye rolled his one eye.

There was the sound of branches breaking underfoot and Dripping Snout burst back through the bushes, snot flying to either side of him. 'Badger Burnhard *will* see you now.'

Horace with McVitie, Loveness, Charlie and Weasel Le Hoop followed Dripping Snout back through the prickly holly bushes, their tough leaves spiking into the foxes' fur and the skin of the snake.

'Ouchy ouch!' Le Hoop yelped as he suffered dozens of tiny cuts.

They trampled through undergrowth and then the ground dipped away into a dark dank ditch at the end of which sat two heavy black hedges.

'I've never seen such a hedge,' Loveness said. 'What is it?'

'Deadly black bay,' Dripping Snout said. 'It's best you don't touch.'

Loveness drew her shoulders in tight so she wouldn't scrape a single leaf as they entered a pitch-black passage. Horace opened his eyes as wide as he could in an effort to see. The ground felt dusty and there was a stink of rotting apples.

The stench made Loveness cough.

'Are you all right?' Horace said.

'No talking,' One Eye said.

Dust was in Horace's throat and he also coughed.

'Shut it!' One Eye said.

Charlie tripped and banged into Horace.

'Watch it,' McVitie whinged.

'Silence!' One Eye ordered.

'Stop! Everyone, stop.' Dripping Snout said. 'Cover your eyes.'

Horace didn't see why he should.

Loveness cried out as Horace yelped and Charlie said, 'Blimey, what is *that?*' Meanwhile McVitie covered his eyes with his tail and Weasel Le Hoop looked away, jittering even more than usual.

'It's too much,' Horace said.

The whole floor was shaking.

'I don't like it,' Loveness said. 'I really don't like it.'

'Follow!' Dripping Snout said.

They followed orders and trooped into a muddy-walled chamber with a floor that crunched underfoot. Slowly, as their eyes grew used to the dark, a huge figure appeared. There, towards the back, in the centre of the space, sat a gargantuan badger with three chins and four bellies resting in front of him on a comfortable mound of earth.

Dripping Snout bowed. 'Your visitors, sir.'

The huge badger picked a feather from his teeth and bit down on a hunk of raw meat. 'I'd offer you some, only it's not in my nature.' He scratched his third and fourth bellies. 'What does fox taste like? Shall I tell you?'

One Eye and Dripping Snout sniggered.

A bitter sickly taste rose in Horace's throat and his stomach gave a violent heave as he thought of the moment his little brother Bert was snatched from the cosy warmth of his home. He bit his lip and cleared his throat. 'I've always been told badgers and foxes need to get along,' he said. 'I was told it's best we respect one another and leave well alone.'

The huge badger looked over their heads. 'Did someone speak? Did I hear an ickle voice? I hope I didn't, because Badger Burnhard listens to no one *and he wants to keep it that way.*' He scratched his backside with his long, razor-sharp claws.

He's clearly mad!

Horace wanted nothing more than to get out, run for it and never return, because he realised that all he cared about was Loveness. He looked across at her and shuffled closer, keen to protect her.

'Who is moving?' Badger Burnhard glared. 'Did I say you could move?'

Horace felt himself blush beneath his fur coat.

'Bring me pigeon!' Burnhard shouted, as he continued to scratch his itchy parts.

Never had Horace met a creature quite so greedy or grotesque. No wonder Burnhard wanted the Strawberry Hill den even though he had the Dark Hedges and another nineteen or more homes besides.

Horace was hot, unbearably hot. The place was too small and confined. He wanted to get out but all he could do was shift on the spot. He felt more crunching underfoot and looked down. There were bones – clean white bones and tiny skulls.

Badger Burnhard smiled as he noticed Horace look at the floor. 'Family, friends, enemies, who knows? I've no room for sentiment.' He kicked at a small skull close to his stubby foot. 'Could be a fox cub, that one.' Badger Burnhard leant forward to scratch a long scar that cut across his lower leg.

A sudden sharp pain shot through Horace's heart.

Wounded paw? Is he the one who took Bert?

A sick taste rose in Horace's throat and he felt ill. He wanted to get out but needed to protect Loveness. He stepped even closer, keen to reassure her, but he was worried. Never before had he met such a monster.

Dripping Snout returned with a pigeon for his boss.

'About time.' Badger Burnhard looked back at the foxes. 'Still warm, just the way I like them. So now you've so rudely invited yourselves over, what is it you want?'

Horace cleared his throat ready to speak, but how to say what he needed to without ending up dead?

Charlie stepped forward. 'We're here about the den left to Horace by his dad,' he said.

'*Shush!* It doesn't matter any more,' Horace said, scared his dear friend Charlie, beautiful Loveness and he himself would be instantly killed.

Badger Burnhard's black eyes glowered. 'Something his dad left to that young rascal? What's that got to do with me? These are the Wild Woods – *my* Wild Woods. We do things differently here.'

Horace considered stepping in and denying it all, but a bigger part of him knew they'd come too far, and why should Badger Burnhard take what was rightfully his? It just wasn't on. The badger was a bully – a big, fat, witches'-toothpaste-striped bully with four bellies, three chins and two scary nut-job eyes.

Ma would say, don't give in, never give in, bullies shouldn't win.

Horace's stomach churned. He was about to do something that would put him in serious danger, but he wasn't concerned for himself – it was Loveness he was worried about. He had promised Claretina to get her home safely. What would happen to Loveness if Horace were killed?

Again Charlie stepped forward, his ears sharp, his chest out and his mouth open, showing his one and a half fangs. 'Badger Burnhard,' he said, 'we've been to Strawberry Hill. We arrived well before the deadline and we are here to claim the den. It is neither yours nor your son's. Its rightful owner is Horace Fox.'

There was a crunching of bones underfoot as Burnhard's bulk shifted. Lifting his chin, he narrowed his eyes to mere slits as he looked down at Charlie and said, 'While my son Selwyn remains living there, the den is mine.'

'But Selwyn's not happy there all on his own,' Charlie said.

'He wants to please you and that's why he's staying, but he'd much rather be here with you, his best and only dad.'

Badger Burnhard curled his lip as he shifted his considerable weight and scratched his buttocks. 'You.' He looked at Charlie. 'You're Horace Fox?'

Horace opened his mouth to speak, but Charlie beat him to it. 'It's me, yes, I'm Horace Fox,' he said, standing firm to face Burnhard's threatening bulk.

McVitie's head jerked up with surprise, his coiled body tightening slightly around Horace's neck.

'Watch it, McVitie!' Horace whispered. 'Don't forget I stuck up for you when One Eye and Dripping Snout made fun of you *and* I peeled you off the road when you were squashed by that car.'

Charlie was still there, standing tall, his chest out and Horace held his breath as once again his dear friend put himself in danger to protect him.

Badger Burnhard hoisted his huge frame to full height. Towering above everyone, he shuffled forward, his thighs rubbing together as he moved up close to Charlie. Sniffing hard, he moved even closer so his small black eyes could take a long hard look. 'You don't look much like him,' he said.

'Like who?'

'Dickie.'

Charlie's expression was blank.

'Your father – Dickie Fox – you look nothing like him.' Burnhard sniffed even harder and again scratched his backside.

Horace held his breath, convinced Charlie's lie was about to be discovered, putting them all in immediate danger.

But Charlie held his nerve. 'Who *do* I look like then?'

'More like that wretched vixen Rosalie – nothing but scabby fox trash.'

How dare he say that?

Horace gritted his teeth as he forced himself to hold back and not react. It was so hard to hear Badger Burnhard insult his ma and yet say nothing.

The air in the dark chamber was heavy, the mood tense. Something had to give.

Badger Burnhard nodded to One Eye and Dripping Snout who were standing facing each other on opposite sides of the room. 'Take them to the pit,' he said.

'What, all of them?' One Eye said.

'All of them.'

'What – even McVitie?'

Badger Burnhard turned towards the snake.

'Please, thir,' McVitie lisped.

Badger Burnhard scowled at the sight of McVitie. 'Without your teeth you're even more *useless* than I thought.' He nodded to One Eye and Dripping Snout. 'Take them all.'

'But, Badger Burnhard, thir, you're forgetting my yearth of thervith and the many, many enemieth I have dethpatched in your honour.'

'You've only ever done something for me if I've given you something in return. Well, it's a pity you failed with the fox or you'd be on your way to a luxury retirement in Scotland at one of my finest Highland properties. But now instead it's the pit where you will remain at my pleasure, and to be honest it *will* give me pleasure to think of you rotting away down there!'

One Eye grabbed Charlie and Loveness, while Dripping Snout went for Horace. Horace, however, was choking.

'What's up with him?' Dripping Snout said.

Horace was gasping for air, his eyes bloodshot and bulging.

'*Oh no!*' Loveness cried. 'Someone do something!'

'What's happening to him?' Dripping Snout said again.

'The snake – it's the snake,' Horace said between gasps.

McVitie had slowly coiled himself around Horace's neck another few times and gradually tightened his grip, constricting his muscular body, slowly squeezing the life out of Horace.

'What are you doing, McVitie?' Badger Burnhard said. 'No one told you to strangle anyone right now.'

McVitie hissed, his forked tongue flickered, and his eyes glowered as he revelled in his deadly squeeze. '*Thith* ith Horath. I brought him to you. It ith I who hath revealed hith true identity. You owe me. I have thucktheeded for you.'

Horace's eyes flipped back in his head and he dropped to the bone-covered floor with an almighty *crunch!*

'*Horace!*' Loveness tried to pull away from One Eye's grip. 'What have you done to him?'

'Is the young fox dead?' Badger Burnhard said.

One Eye relaxed his grip on Charlie and Loveness so he could kneel and check Horace for signs of life. Charlie saw his chance and leapt at Burnhard, biting his snout and holding on tight as the out-of-shape badger flailed about in a vain attempt to release himself.

Weasel Le Hoop, not known for his bravery, was so angry at McVitie's treachery that he in turn bit the snake's tail.

Dripping Snout and One Eye turned on Charlie and swinging their heavy paws swiped at him and bit as they tried to tear him off their master.

While all this was going on, Loveness and Le Hoop quietly pulled Horace out of Badger Burnhard's dark bone-covered chamber.

'We can do this,' Loveness said as she gently pawed his face. 'Come on, Horace, wake up!'

Horace's right eyelid flickered.

'He's alive!' Loveness said, with tears in her beautiful eyes.

'Quick, let's get him out of here,' said Weasel Le Hoop, and they pulled Horace through the Dark Hedges, past the wall of holly and back into the leafy ditch.

'Where's Charlie?' Horace moaned.

Loveness looked at Le Hoop, unsure of what to say.

'We can't leave without Charlie,' Horace said. 'We have to go back in.'

'I was afraid you'd say that,' said Weasel Le Hoop.

Something swooped low over their heads.

Looking up, they saw a tawny owl on a branch above them, the same one they'd seen before. 'There's another way,' she said. 'I'll show you – follow me.' The owl took off, flying low and steady around the side of the wall of holly trees, and then between tall bare tree trunks into a clearing.

Loveness and Weasel Le Hoop kept up, while Horace dragged behind as best he could.

'What's this?' said Le Hoop. 'There's nothing here.'

'Look,' the owl said. 'Look closer.'

There was a small ditch on the other side of the clearing, full of brown rotting leaves.

'You mean that?' Horace asked.

The owl nodded.

Horace staggered towards the ditch. He was still dizzy and needed to rest but there was no time for recovery so he jumped straight in and instantly disappeared into the leaves as if he'd stepped in quicksand.

'What is this – a trick?' Loveness said. 'What have you done?'

'Why would I trick you?' the owl said. 'It's in my own interests to be rid of Badger Burnhard. He takes my babies – always, always, he takes my precious owlets.'

At that moment, Horace's head peeked out from the leaves. 'It's another entrance. We can take them by surprise.' Burrowing back down, he disappeared again, and Loveness and Weasel Le Hoop followed him into a long dark tunnel.

'What's that on the walls?' Loveness said.

Horace felt the wall with his nose. 'Feels soft, like feathers.'

'I dread to think why that's there,' Loveness said. 'That maniac needs to be stopped.'

They skulked forward in the dark.

'It's getting warmer,' Loveness said. 'We must be nearly there.'

'I can't do this,' said Le Hoop.

It grew warmer and warmer still until they reached a dark round chamber. They felt around the walls with their noses. There were two tunnels leading out.

'Which one?' Loveness said.

Horace chose the exit on the left, feeling his way along the tunnel which led back to Burnhard's lair. Once again, the evil badger was eating – always eating.

Dripping Snout came into view.

'The fox is in the pit, sir,' he said.

'You two are useless. We've only got one of them.' Badger Burnhard shook his head and scratched his many chins. 'I fancy an owlet but it's the wrong season. Get me slugs – a big mound of juicy slugs – and make it snappy.'

Dripping Snout turned towards the tunnel where Horace was hiding.

Immediately Horace backed up the tunnel and out. 'Other exit, quick!' he told the others.

'It's another tunnel,' Loveness said.

'We've got to take it,' Horace said. 'Let me go first.' Skulking low, he followed the passage to another chamber and as the darkness lifted, they found themselves teetering on the edge of a large black pit.

'Hello!' Horace said. 'Anybody down there?'

'*Horace, it's me – Charlie!*'

'What is this place?' Horace said.

'It's a hole of horrors, full of bones and skulls. Mate, you've got to get me out of here.'

'We'll have to dig and push earth down until you can climb up.'

It was a risky plan – if too much mud collapsed in on Charlie, he could be buried alive, but there was no other choice.

Horace, Loveness and Weasel Le Hoop set to work, scraping at the hardened mud until the edges began to collapse in on the hole.

'Not too fast!' Charlie shouted, as the mud showered down on him.

Meanwhile Zigzag McVitie silently slithered into the dark chamber, saw what was going on and slithered out again.

The alarm had been raised.

Deep down in the pit, Charlie patted the mud down bit by bit to form a ramp that would allow him to escape. 'Stop!' he said, when at last he knew he could make it out. He trotted up the ramp, muddy but smiling from ear to ear, just as Dripping Snout and One Eye appeared, blocking the entrances to both exit tunnels.

'*Ankles!*' Horace shouted and dived at One Eye's right leg while Charlie went for the left one, and Loveness and Weasel Le Hoop attacked Dripping Snout.

'*Aargh!*' yelled the badgers, as they tried to shake the foxes off.

One Eye growled and lashed out, his yellow teeth gnashing the air. Horace bit down hard and trying to get away, Dripping Snout fell into the pit.

'Stand clear! One Eye's going too,' said Le Hoop, as the hulking badger crashed down on his friend.

The foxes and weasel kicked at the earth to break down the muddy ramp Charlie had built.

'Let's get out of here,' Loveness said.

They knew only too well that the pit with its partial ramp would not hold the badgers back for long.

And so they left, without any agreement from Badger Burnhard that the Strawberry Hill den belonged to Horace. It felt like failure and yet they were all still alive. Horace, Charlie, Loveness and Weasel Le Hoop came out of the tunnel and into the ditch.

The owl swooped in low over their heads. 'Where do you need to go? I'll guide you.'

'Take me home to Ma,' Loveness said.

Horace smiled. 'Yes, take us back to Strawberry Hill.'

Eighteen

The thin sliver of moon had disappeared behind heavy cloud and the sky was empty of stars as they followed the owl back to Strawberry Hill.

'There it is.' Horace was once again wide-eyed as its towers and castle-like outline came into view, their perfect creamy whiteness glowing against the dark sky.

The owl took them as far as the gates. 'I'll leave you now.' She flew up, only to dive down within seconds to take out a mouse.

Horace's stomach rumbled.

Loveness said, 'Horace, have I done something to offend you?'

'Of course not! Whatever gave you that idea?'

'You're growling.'

'It's his stomach,' Charlie said. 'He's a nightmare if he doesn't get fed.'

'What are we going to do now?' Weasel Le Hoop said. 'We're still on a mission, aren't we?'

'Are we?' Horace said.

Le Hoop made a face and said, 'Well, I don't see you settled in your own cosy den.'

Horace nodded. 'It's time to come up with Plan B.'

'What about Ma?' Loveness said. 'She'll be worrying about me.'

Horace nodded. 'We'll go and see Claretina before we do anything else.'

The foxes went through a hole under the fence into the grounds of Strawberry Hill, then ran across the lawns and past the big old oak tree that sat over the occupied den.

'Hello, house,' Horace said, waving his tail. 'Don't worry, I'll be back soon, I promise. I'm coming for you.'

'Yeah, and this time we're *all* going in,' Charlie said.

Keen to see her ma, Loveness ran ahead and jumped through the foxhole into the overgrown orchard before slowing a little as she neared the rough old shed over the den. She squeezed her head into the entrance hidden at the side.

'Ma, it's me! I'm back.'

'Loveness, my sweet.' Claretina nuzzled her daughter's furry cheek. 'Dearie me, just look at you. You must all be so hungry.' Claretina dug in a corner where she'd buried a stash of mice and a large pile of nachos. 'I've had a good day's hunting and scavenging.' She set the food out on the ground to share and the foxes and weasel got to work in their usual manic feeding frenzy. Within seconds, all that was left was a small pile of bones, some gristle and a few crumbs.

Their bellies full, Horace, Charlie, Loveness, Claretina and Le Hoop then went out to drink from the old water butt at the side of the shed before carrying on out of the orchard, back through the foxhole and into the grounds of Strawberry Hill House.

Scurrying along the fence at the edge, they flitted from bush to bush until they arrived at the largest oak tree. Bones and scraps of food littered the ground around the blocked-up entrance. Selwyn had well and truly made himself at home.

Horace bristled as he stared up at the starless sky.

'Pity it's been so cold lately,' Claretina said, 'or we could dig.'

'What's that, Ma?' Loveness said.

'Well, if the ground were soft, we could simply dig underneath to make a new entrance. Badger Selwyn can't guard two openings at the same time.'

Horace's mouth fell open. 'Why didn't I think of that? Claretina, you've given me my Plan B – we'll dig!'

'You'll never be able to dig now though,' Claretina said. 'The ground's too hard.'

'It depends how much you want something,' Horace said, 'and I really do want this home that should be mine.'

Charlie scraped at the hard earth. 'Come on, let's form a digging party.'

It was likely to take hours, maybe all night. And there would be injuries – sore paws and broken claws. Claretina organised snacks to keep them going: nuts, apples and everyone's favourite rat-tailed maggots, all washed down with big gulps of pond water.

'Did you feel that?' Horace looked up suddenly, his mouth open in a wide foxy grin as he held out his tongue. 'It's raining!'

Water splashed onto Charlie's nose and Loveness's tail and soon turned into a full-on downpour.

Claretina shook her head. 'I don't believe it – you are one lucky fox, Horace!'

Charlie scraped at the ground. 'It's softening up already.'

Horace, head down, clawed at the earth, flinging soft squidgy mud behind him as he edged slowly down, squeezing in between the roots of the tree to avoid harming the ancient oak.

'This is it! This is my home. We're breaking through.' Horace scooped out another pawful of earth and then broke through into what felt like a large hole. He peered in but it was hard to see anything in the darkness, so he dug a little more.

The rain eased off, the clouds lifted and moonlight flooded the space.

His heart beating fast, Horace squeezed in, followed by the

others.

Circling the space, he found a homely chamber that was both warm and roomy. But where was Badger Selwyn? Horace held his breath. There were three black holes leading off this area. He waited a moment for his eyes to grow used to the darkness.

'Let's split up and each of us take a tunnel,' Horace said.

Charlie nodded. 'We'll swarm that spoilt thieving badger.'

Horace, Charlie and Loveness each picked a tunnel while Weasel Le Hoop and Claretina remained in the first chamber.

Edging forward, Horace found the ground dipping gently into a further space. He paused, blinking in the darkness. 'Hello,' he said. 'Badger Selwyn, are you there? Show yourself. We need to talk.'

There was a crunch, a whoosh and then Horace's feet were kicked out from under him.

Taken by surprise, Horace yelped and fell onto his back as Badger Selwyn went for his throat.

'Get off me, you brute!' Horace cried, fighting back.

Badger and fox rolled as one as Selwyn snapped again and again at Horace's throat while Horace kicked out at the badger's soft belly.

No, this place is mine! You have no right.

Horace felt an almighty strength rise up inside him, and pushing up, shoved Badger Selwyn away with his shoulder.

Snarling, Horace spat and bared his teeth, his front fangs long, sharp and deadly. 'It's time for you to get out,' he said. 'It's over, Selwyn. Your dad doesn't own this place, he never has. It belonged to my dad, Dickie, and now it's mine.'

Badger Selwyn froze, a confused look on his face, his wide-apart eyes looking in opposite directions. 'But my daddy owns everything – all the dens, all the setts, all the burrows. Badger Burnhard rules the Dark Hedges and the Wild Woods and way beyond, as far as the Highlands of Scotland.'

'This den is nothing to do with your dad. It belonged to my dad, Dickie, and he passed it on to me – it's what foxes do. It's time for you to do the decent thing and leave now, Selwyn.'

'Why should I?'

Horace shook his head and said, 'Because even your dad agrees it's not his to take. He knows that – he admitted it himself.'

Badger Selwyn scratched his head and backside, both at the same time. 'Did you go and see my dad?'

'Yep.'

'What did he say?'

'He wants you home with him. You're his special boy.'

'He said that?' Badger Selwyn's eyes glistened. 'I'd like to go home.'

Charlie and Loveness arrived, their hackles up and mouths open – teeth bared, ready to fight.

'Where are we at?' Charlie said. 'Tell me where we're at and we'll act superfast and super deadly.'

'Let me at him, that thieving badger,' Loveness said. 'I'll show him!'

'Selwyn is just leaving,' Horace said.

Charlie looked confused for a moment. 'Oh, I see . . . Right. Well, in that case, I'll show him out.'

Charlie escorted Badger Selwyn off the premises. 'And don't come back!' he said, giving Selwyn a quick shove up the backside. 'You're not welcome here.'

Claretina watched Badger Selwyn exit through the ditch they'd dug under the fence. He grumbled a little and scratched his furry rear before hunching his shoulders and plodding off in the direction of the Dark Hedges.

'Off you go, son,' Claretina said. 'Your dad's waiting for you.'

'We should have finished him off,' Charlie said.

But Horace disagreed. 'I couldn't take a father's son.' He thought back to when Bert was taken and how the loss had changed everything. 'Claretina, there's one thing I don't understand,' he said, as he thought of his ma's beloved den in a ditch on scrubland by the railway track and how happy they had all once been. 'How come my dad ended up here so far from home?'

'Your dad was a good fox,' she said. 'Dickie and Rosalie adored one another but it's so hard to lose a son. Dickie couldn't help but blame himself for Bert's death, saying he should have been there, while your ma blamed herself, saying she should have fought to the death. They argued and Dickie left. He went in search of Badger Burnhard and one night he tracked him down to the Dark Hedges. There was an almighty struggle and then Dickie had Burnhard by the throat. Dickie had only to bite down a fraction and that would have been it for Burnhard. The badger was pleading for mercy but Dickie didn't care – he was ready to finish it. And you know the only thing that stopped him?

'Burnhard's son, Selwyn, happened to wander in. He was small then, barely talking. He gurgled a bit and Dickie eased off. He thought of Bert and he just couldn't do it. He couldn't leave the cub without a dad.

'Dickie left the Dark Hedges after that, but he told Burnhard he'd remain close by, watching him, and if he put a paw wrong he'd be back and he'd finish it next time.'

'And Badger Burnhard stayed away?'

'Yes, while Dickie was alive, but ever since your dad passed, Badger Burnhard has taken no end of dens, setts and burrows. He just can't get enough of food and property.'

'Well, at least I've claimed what is rightfully mine,' said Horace.

'Yes, it's a good start. Hopefully others will do the same,' Claretina said.

'I think it's time I looked around.'

This time they went in by the front entrance to the den.

'This is the main living area,' Claretina said, as they found themselves in a large round space with mud walls and a floor of soft dry oak leaves.

Horace brushed his tail along the wall. 'It feels like home.' He pushed his nose into the leaves on the floor. 'It could even smell like home once the scent of Badger Selwyn has gone.'

He poked his nose into the three chambers leading off the main area – all cosy and well built. One had several old gardening gloves that would make a fine pillow; another had a tartan wool picnic blanket. 'I like this!' Horace said. 'It reminds me of that old stick who left out meat with jelly in a silver dish.'

There was also a half-chewed flip-flop, a cuddly lion and a tennis ball.

'What a great collection!' Horace said.

In the final chamber lay a soft carpet of oak leaves and a scent Horace instantly recognised. 'Do you smell that?' He scurried around the edge, sniffing closer, then dug a little under the leaves and pulled out a small lock of orangey-red fur. 'Do you smell that, Charlie?' There were tears in his eyes.

'Yes, I smell it.'

The lock of fur smelt of home. It smelt of the ditch on scrubland by the railway track. And most of all, it smelt of his dear old ma, Rosalie.

'How come this is here?' Horace said.

'Dickie brought it with him,' Claretina said.

'And kept it by his bedside all this time,' Loveness said.

Horace thought of the fur he'd left caught on the wire as he'd squeezed through the fence along the edge of Ma's territory. Maybe Ma had once done the same and his dad had found a tuft of her fur as he left, and taken it so he would always have something of her with him?

'He never stopped loving her,' Claretina said.

'So why didn't he come back to us?'

'He planned to but he broke his leg. He was lame and had to take time out to let it heal. There was no way he could have made it back until he had returned to fitness. Anyway, the leg did mend though it was never quite the same, and he did set off, but—'

'What happened?'

'He was found by the roadside.'

'Run over?'

'I don't think so.'

'What then?'

'He missed your ma so much. I think he was afraid to go back, afraid Rosalie might have found someone new, or rather someone new might have found her.' Claretina looked down and sighed. 'He looked perfect when we found him. There wasn't a scratch to be seen.'

'So what was it?'

'He died of a broken heart,' Loveness said.

Horace frowned. 'I don't get it.'

'His worst fear was that he'd make it back to your ma's den in the ditch on the scrubland by the railway track and that none of you would be there. He knew time was running out and that you boys would all be moving away. Maybe the pressure just got too much for him.'

Charlie sighed and said, 'It sounds like a heart attack to me.'

Horace plopped down amongst the leaves and stared down at his paws. His tail was as low as it would go. 'I don't know. I do like this place but it's not home. Home is with my ma and my sisters, Kitty and May.'

Loveness's tail dipped low too as she listened, watching Horace with her light amber eyes.

Charlie curled his lip, showing his chipped left fang. 'Are

you telling me we went on this whole crazy great river quest to claim this rather swanky den here and now you don't even want it? You're having a laugh, right?'

Weasel Le Hoop stood up, sat down, stood up again.

'Stop fidgeting, Le Hoop!' Charlie said.

'I can't help it, sorry.' Le Hoop looked at Horace. 'The thing is . . . you're here now.'

Charlie nodded. 'Some foxes don't know how lucky they are.'

'And the truth is, we foxes have to leave home,' Claretina said. 'We all have to travel far and wide and make our own way in the world.'

'It's what foxes do,' Loveness said.

'Exactly,' Claretina said. 'It's time for you to make your own life now, Horace, maybe even start a family of your own here in this wonderful den your dad left to you.'

Horace took a deep breath. It was a lot to take in. He looked around at his friends new and old – from Charlie Boom to Weasel Le Hoop, Claretina and his dear Loveness.

He had a lump in his throat. 'I've spent so long concentrating on the home I lost that I haven't been able to see the one I've gained.' He stroked the mud walls and the carpet of soft oak leaves. 'It's beautiful here, and what great neighbours I'll have!' He smiled at Loveness and Claretina. 'It's such a big den, larger than I need, with plenty of room for visitors.' He thought of his ma, Rosalie, and his sisters, Kitty and May. 'And there's plenty of room for friends!' He grinned at Charlie and Le Hoop. 'You're right, this is my new home. It's what foxes do and I am one lucky fox.'

With Charlie's help, Horace swept the den clean, clearing out bones and other rubbish left by Badger Selwyn, while keeping Dickie's special treasures and the precious tuft of Ma's fur.

That evening they celebrated, joined by Weasel Le Hoop,

Claretina and Loveness. But, after a shared feast of turkey leftovers, chipolatas and cake, Charlie grew restless.

'What is it?' Horace asked, noticing his friend's change of mood. 'Is it Zigzag McVitie or Badger Burnhard? Have they come back to reclaim my home?' He scanned the surrounding bushes for any sign of movement.

'It's not that, don't worry,' Charlie said, 'it's just that I need to get back, check my own territory, know what I mean?'

Horace's tail dropped low. 'I thought you'd stay.'

'Mate, this is your place. I'm a city type, you know that.'

Horace looked down at his paws. 'It won't be the same without you.'

'I'll come and visit. In fact, the first thing I'm going to do is pop over to your ma's ditch and let her know you're all right.'

Horace's tail remained low as he waved his friend goodbye.

'He'll be back to visit with your ma and sisters before you know it,' Claretina said to comfort him.

Horace thought of how Charlie would guide Ma, Kitty and May through the city and along the river to visit him at Strawberry Hill. They'd be safe with Charlie, and in the meantime he'd keep himself busy.

'I'd like to try the food at all the local takeaways,' he said.

'I know all the best places to go,' Loveness said.

'Will you show me where to find them?'

Loveness smiled. 'Horace, we will dine our way around the world!' She talked of wondrous-sounding places: Time for Thai, Club Mexicana and Little Mumbai. 'It's all here and in skulking distance,' she said. 'Sushi, pizza, noodles, fried chicken – you name it, we can eat it.'

They arranged to meet the following day as soon as the sticks had gone indoors, but long before anyone came to empty the bins. They'd eat out and then chill in the magic hour before sunrise.

What will it be – Indian, Chinese, Turkish, French, Lebanese, Italian or Japanese?

The options seemed endless, Horace thought, as his stomach rumbled and groaned.

So much to look forward to . . .

Heading back inside, he pawed at the soft dried oak leaves lining the floor of his very swish den.

What a place! Don't I always come through in the end?

Making himself comfortable, he settled for a nap, happy to finally have a place of his own.

Acknowledgements

Thank you to my editor and friend Monica Byles whose enthusiasm and eagle-eye for mistakes and inconsistencies makes her a joy to work with.

To all my writer friends who read extracts from earlier versions – Linda Buckley-Archer, Kyo Choi, Christabel Cooper, Kate Harrison, Dominique Jackson, Jacqui Lofthouse, EJ Swift, Colin Tucker, Louise Voss, and Stephanie Zia – thanks for your ongoing support.

Mark Mason Gardner's wonderful photographs of the foxes that visit his urban garden and the name of his Instagram (@foxnthecity) and Facebook account Fox N The City were an inspiration.

Illustrating this book proved a good way to cope with lockdown and I'm grateful to my partner Daryl and our daughters Zanzi and Bijou who all seem to understand my obsession with foxes.

About the Author

Jacqui Hazell is the award-winning author of *My Life as a Bench*. Born near Portsmouth, she studied textile design at Nottingham and has an MA in creative writing from Royal Holloway, University of London. She lives in London with her partner, their two daughters and a small dog called Basil who is as close as she can get to having a fox of her own.

Horace Fox in the City is the first in a new series of books by Jacqui Hazell. Watch out for the next title, coming soon!

To find out more, visit her website at www.jacquihazell.com

For young adults

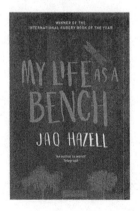

Made in the USA
Monee, IL
01 February 2021

59341820R00104